AF441008

Eyes On Me

Blind Sight Series, Volume 3

Lexy Timms

Published by Dark Shadow Publishing, 2020.

This is a work of fiction. Similarities to real people, places, or events are entirely coincidental.

EYES ON ME

First edition. March 11, 2020.

Copyright © 2020 Lexy Timms.

Written by Lexy Timms.

Also by Lexy Timms

A Bad Boy Bullied Romance
I Hate You
I Hate You A Little Bit
I Hate You A Little Bit More

A Burning Love Series
Spark of Passion
Flame of Desire
Blaze of Ecstasy

A Chance at Forever Series
Forever Perfect
Forever Desired
Forever Together

A Dating App Series
I've Been Matched
You've Been Matched

We've Been Matched

A "Kind of" Billionaire
Taking a Risk
Safety in Numbers
Pretend You're Mine

A Maybe Series
Maybe I Should
Maybe I Shouldn't
Maybe I Did

BBW Romance Series
Capturing Her Beauty
Pursuing Her Dreams
Tracing Her Curves

Beating the Biker Series
Making Her His
Making the Break
Making of Them

Billionaire Banker Series
Banking on Him

Price of Passion
Investing in Love
Knowing Your Worth
Treasured Forever
Banking on Christmas

Billionaire Holiday Romance Series
Driving Home for Christmas
The Valentine Getaway
Cruising Love

Billionaire in Disguise Series
Facade
Illusion
Charade

Billionaire Secrets Series
The Secret
Freedom
Courage
Trust
Impulse
Billionaire Secrets Box Set Books #1-3

Blind Sight Series
See Me

Fix Me
Eyes On Me

Branded Series
Money or Nothing
What People Say
Give and Take

Building Billions
Building Billions - Part 1
Building Billions - Part 2
Building Billions - Part 3

Change of Heart Series
The Heart Needs
The Heart Wants
The Heart Knows

Conquering Warrior Series
Ruthless

Counting the Billions
Counting the Days
Counting On You

Counting the Kisses

Diamond in the Rough Anthology
Billionaire Rock
Billionaire Rock - part 2

Dirty Little Taboo Series
Flirting Touch
Denying Pleasure
Forbidding Desire
Craving Passion

Dominating PA Series
Her Personal Assistant - Part 1
Her Personal Assistant Box Set

Fake Billionaire Series
Faking It
Temporary CEO
Caught in the Act
Never Tell A Lie
Fake Christmas
Fake Billionaire Box Set #1-3

Firehouse Romance Series
Caught in Flames
Burning With Desire
Craving the Heat
Firehouse Romance Complete Collection

Forging Billions Series
Dirty Money
Petty Cash
Payment Required

For His Pleasure
Elizabeth
Georgia
Madison

Fortune Riders MC Series
Billionaire Biker
Billionaire Ransom
Billionaire Misery

Fragile Series
Fragile Touch
Fragile Kiss

Fragile Love

Great Temptation Series
The Devil's Footsteps
Heaven's Command
Mortals Surrender

Hades' Spawn Motorcycle Club
One You Can't Forget
One That Got Away
One That Came Back
One You Never Leave
One Christmas Night
Hades' Spawn MC Complete Series

Hard Rocked Series
Rhyme
Harmony
Lyrics

Heart of Stone Series
The Protector
The Guardian
The Warrior

Heart of the Battle Series
Celtic Viking
Celtic Rune
Celtic Mann
Heart of the Battle Series Box Set

Heistdom Series
Master Thief
Goldmine
Diamond Heist
Smile For Me
Your Move
Green With Envy
Saving Money

Highlander Wolf Series
Pack Run
Pack Land
Pack Rules

How To Love A Spy
The Secret
The Secret Life
The Secret Wife

Just About Series
About Love
About Truth
About Forever

Justice Series
Seeking Justice
Finding Justice
Chasing Justice
Pursuing Justice
Justice - Complete Series

Kissed by Billions
Kissed by Passion
Kissed by Desire
Kissed by Love

Leaning Towards Trouble
Trouble
Discord
Tenacity

Love You Series
Love Life

Need Love
My Love

Managing the Billionaire
Never Enough
Worth the Cost
Secret Admirers
Chasing Affection
Pressing Romance
Timeless Memories

Managing the Bosses Series
The Boss
The Boss Too
Who's the Boss Now
Love the Boss
I Do the Boss
Wife to the Boss
Employed by the Boss
Brother to the Boss
Senior Advisor to the Boss
Forever the Boss
Christmas With the Boss
Billionaire in Control
Billionaire Makes Millions
Billionaire at Work
Precious Little Thing
Priceless Love
Valentine Love
The Cost of Freedom

Trick or Treat
Gift for the Boss - Novella 3.5
Managing the Bosses Box Set #1-3

Model Mayhem Series
Shameless
Modesty
Imperfection

Moment in Time
Highlander's Bride
Victorian Bride
Modern Day Bride
A Royal Bride
Forever the Bride

My Best Friend's Sister
Hometown Calling
A Perfect Moment
Thrown in Together

My Darker Side Series
Darkest Hour
Time to Stop
Against the Light

Neverending Dream Series
Neverending Dream - Part 1
Neverending Dream - Part 2
Neverending Dream - Part 3
Neverending Dream - Part 4
Neverending Dream - Part 5

Outside the Octagon
Submit
Fight
Knockout

Protecting Diana Series
Her Bodyguard
Her Defender
Her Champion
Her Protector
Her Forever

Protecting Layla Series
His Mission
His Objective
His Devotion

Racing Hearts Series
Rush
Pace
Fast

Regency Romance Series
The Duchess Scandal - Part 1
The Duchess Scandal - Part 2

Reverse Harem Series
Primals
Archaic
Unitary

RIP Series
Track the Ripper
Hunt the Ripper
Pursue the Ripper

R&S Rich and Single Series
Alex Reid
Parker

Saving Forever

Saving Forever - Part 1

Saving Forever - Part 2

Saving Forever - Part 3

Saving Forever - Part 4

Saving Forever - Part 5

Saving Forever - Part 6

Saving Forever Part 7

Saving Forever - Part 8

Saving Forever Boxset Books #1-3

Shifting Desires Series

Jungle Heat

Jungle Fever

Jungle Blaze

Sin Series

Payment for Sin

Atonement Within

Declaration of Love

Southern Romance Series

Little Love Affair

Siege of the Heart

Freedom Forever

Soldier's Fortune

Spanked Series
Passion
Playmate
Pleasure

Spelling Love Series
The Author
The Book Boyfriend
The Words of Love

Taboo Wedding Series
He Loves Me Not
With This Ring
Happily Ever After

Tattooist Series
Confession of a Tattooist
Surrender of a Tattooist
Heart of a Tattooist
Hopes & Dreams of a Tattooist

Tennessee Romance
Whisky Lullaby
Whisky Melody

The Golden Mail
Hot Off the Press
Extra! Extra!
Read All About It
Stop the Press
Breaking News
This Just In

The Lucky Billionaire Series
Lucky Break
Streak of Luck
Lucky in Love

The Sound of Breaking Hearts Series
Disruption
Destroy
Devoted

The University of Gatica Series
The Recruiting Trip
Faster
Higher
Stronger
Dominate
No Rush
University of Gatica - The Complete Series

T.N.T. Series
Troubled Nate Thomas - Part 1
Troubled Nate Thomas - Part 2
Troubled Nate Thomas - Part 3

Undercover Series
Perfect For Me
Perfect For You
Perfect For Us

Unknown Identity Series
Unknown
Unpublished
Unexposed
Unsure
Unwritten
Unknown Identity Box Set: Books #1-3

Unlucky Series
Unlucky in Love
UnWanted
UnLoved Forever

War Torn Letters Series

My Sweetheart
My Darling
My Beloved

Wet & Wild Series
Stormy Love
Savage Love
Secure Love

Worth It Series
Worth Billions
Worth Every Cent
Worth More Than Money

You & Me - A Bad Boy Romance
Just Me
Touch Me
Kiss Me

Standalone
Wash
Loving Charity
Summer Lovin'
Love & College
Billionaire Heart
First Love

Frisky and Fun Romance Box Collection
Beating Hades' Bikers

Watch for more at www.lexytimms.com.

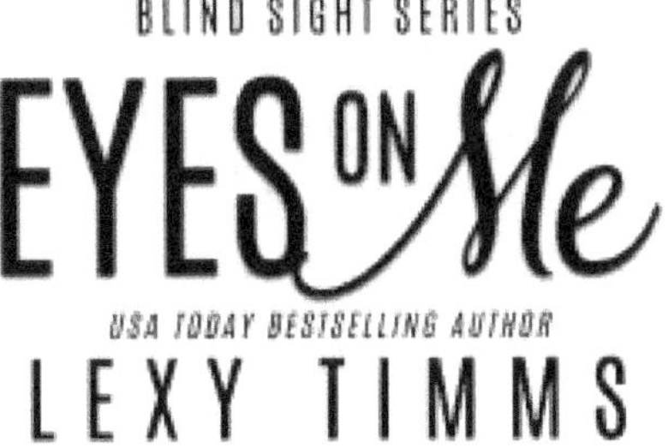

Copyright 2020

1

ALL RIGHTS RESERVED. No part of this publication may be reproduced, stored in or introduced into a retrieval system, or transmitted, in any form, or by any means (electronic, mechanical, photocopying, recording, or otherwise) without the prior written permission of both the copyright owner and the above publisher of this book.

This is a work of fiction. Names, characters, places, brands, media, and incidents are either the product of the author's imagination or are used fictitiously. Any resemblance to an actual person, living or dead, events, or locales is entirely coincidental. The author acknowledges the trademarked status and trademark owners of various products referenced in this work of fiction, which have been used without permission. The publication/use of these trademarks is not authorized, associated with, or sponsored by the trademark owners.

All rights reserved.
Eyes On Me
Blind Sight Series #3
Copyright 2020 by Lexy Timms
Cover by: Book Cover by Design[1]

Blind Sight Series

Book 1 – See Me
Book 2 – Fix Me
Book 3 – Eyes on Me

Find Lexy Timms:

LEXY TIMMS NEWSLETTER:
http://eepurl.com/9i0vD
Lexy Timms Facebook Page:
https://www.facebook.com/SavingForever
Lexy Timms Website:
http://www.lexytimms.com

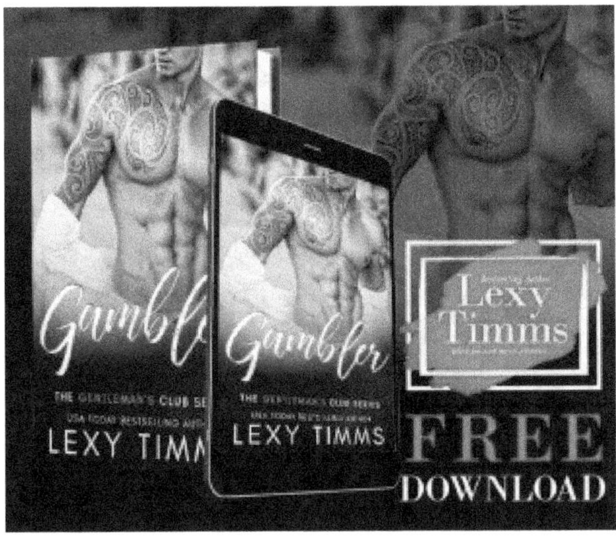
Gambler
THE GENTLEMAN'S CLUB SERIES
USA TODAY BESTSELLING AUTHOR
LEXY TIMMS
Gambler
THE GENTLEMAN'S CLUB SERIES
LEXY TIMMS
Lexy Timms
FREE
DOWNLOAD

Want to read more...
For **FREE**?
Sign up for Lexy Timms' newsletter
And she'll send you updates on new releases, ARC copies of books
and a whole lotta fun!
Sign up for news and updates!
http://eepurl.com/9i0vD

Eyes On Me Blurb:

"SOMETIMES THE HEART sees what is invisible to the eye."

Bree Sullivan was never a risk-taker. When a chance at true happiness has her stepping outside her comfort-zone, taking the leap blindly is what she's doing—literally. But this leap is a surgery that may help her see again.

With Luke at her side, she does the surgery and the recovery and results are agonizingly slow, threating to pull her into a deep depression.

What if she never sees again? What if things don't work out for her and Luke?

More terrifying, what if they do?

Chapter One

Bree

MY BODY FELT HEAVY, weighted down but completely relaxed. I could hear the soft beep mingled with low murmurs. For a brief moment, I was confused about where I was. Consciousness gradually returned, bringing me up from the shadowy depths I had been submerged in. I moved my fingers before lifting my hand. There was something on my face.

"Hey there," I heard Luke's voice.

"Luke?" I questioned. Just before my hand could touch my face, he grabbed it with his.

"You need to leave the bandages on," he said.

"Bandages?" I asked with confusion.

"Your surgery is over, but you'll need to wear the bandages for a few hours. Dr. Tanner will be in to check on you a little while."

"Did it work?" I asked. The question felt so much bigger than three simple words. My entire future depended on what the answer to that question was. I was almost afraid to know.

"I'm sure it did, but we won't know until Ellis gets here," he answered.

I liked when he called her Ellis. It made it feel like she was a friend and not a doctor with no true vested interest. While I was jealous of the woman, I did like her and appreciated her kindness. If the surgery worked, I owed her so much more than a thank you. I owed her every-thing.

"Where's my dad?" I asked.

"He went down to the coffee shop to get us a couple coffees. I would offer you some, but the nurse said you couldn't have anything until she said so and she terrifies me, so we are going to listen to her."

I offered a smile. "Have you been here the whole time?"

"You know it. I used my nursing credentials to sweet talk them into letting us come into recovery."

"I bet you used a lot more than that."

He chuckled. "I am not above flirting a little if it means I get to be with you. How are you feeling?"

"My throat is a little sore and I feel a little groggy, but other than that, fine. Except the blackness. I really didn't want to see nothing."

"She warned you it would take a few weeks before your vision was restored," he said.

I sighed, fighting back the despair. "But I thought I would see something."

"You might. She'll be in soon and will explain everything. Don't give up hope. Not yet. You've come this far."

I touched the bandages that were taped to my eyes. "I don't like this," I told him. "I don't like the way it feels."

"It won't be long," he said. "Remember, she told you this would be temporary. You'll have them off tomorrow. Maybe even earlier."

"You're awake," my father's voice cut into the room.

"Hi Dad."

"How do you feel?" he asked.

"Blind," I muttered.

"Bree," he said, my name and I knew exactly what he was going to say.

I held up a hand, only to have the IV that was in the back of my hand pull a bit. "Don't say it. I already know I have to wait. How long?"

"You've only been out of surgery for about thirty minutes," Luke pointed out. "Ellis said she would be around a couple hours after you were alert."

I groaned. I didn't want to wait another minute. I felt like I had been waiting my entire life. My life was on hold until I knew one way or another if the surgery was a success. I had been told it might only be one eye that worked, or I might only get partial vision. I told myself I would be happy with anything. Any little bit of sight would be better than nothing at all. That's what I told myself, but in reality, I wanted it all. I wanted to see the world with twenty-twenty vision again. I wanted to see color. I wanted to see Luke.

Luke and my father spent the next two hours trying to distract me. I hated the bandages on my face. It made me feel so much more claustrophobic than not being able to see in general. I hoped she didn't expect me to wear the damn things throughout the recovery. I was sure I would go crazy if she said I had to.

"Knock, knock," I heard Ellis say.

I immediately sat up a little higher in the bed. I was unhooked from the IVs and felt good. I was ready to go home but everything was riding on what happened in the next few minutes. "We're ready," I said, cutting right to the chase. "Do you think it worked?"

"I don't see why it wouldn't have. Are you ready to have the bandages removed?"

I furiously nodded. "Yes!"

She laughed. "Luke can you close the door and turn the lights off?"

I heard him move and heard the door closing. "Why?" I asked, suddenly worried I was going to be maimed and she didn't want to scare patients outside my room.

"Imagine you've spent the last few months in a dark cave. Your eyes need time to adjust. I have a pair of very stylish sunglasses you will need to wear at all times."

I grimaced. "Like those giant square ones?"

She laughed. "Yep. The kind grandpas love to wear. Your eyes will adjust with time. It will be about two weeks, possibly longer before you will feel comfortable enough to be inside a room without them on. You might have sensitivity to sunlight for longer. Always, always, always wear sunglasses when you are outside."

I nodded, anxious to get this show on the road. It wouldn't matter if I wore sunglasses if the surgery didn't work. "Okay."

"Alright, I'm going to remove the bandage."

The familiar saying, 'you could have heard a pin drop' came to mind. I swear my dad and Luke were holding their breath. I sure was. Not to mention that I was also on the verge of throwing up. My anxiety was through the roof. A million thoughts raced through my mind. What would I do first? I wanted to paint. I wanted to go to the beach. I wanted to see Luke.

I stayed perfectly still, letting her unwrap the gauze from around my head. I didn't even care that my hair probably looked horrible. "Is it off?" I asked.

"Yes," Ellis answered. "It's dark in here but there is still some light. Go ahead and open your eyes."

Honestly, I didn't even realize I had them closed. I took a deep breath, steeling my nerves, promising myself I wouldn't freak out when there was nothing but blackness in front of me. I cracked them open just a fraction. There was nothing. My heart nearly stopped beating as I slowly opened them all the way.

Blinking several times, I was surprised that my eyes hurt, which I suppose was understandable given what had just happened. "I don't see anything," I whispered, despair washing over me.

"Give it a few seconds," Ellis calmly answered. "Your brain needs to adjust to the sensory input. Do you see light?"

That's when it hit me. I did see light! "Yes!" I practically screamed. "I can't see anything, but I see shadows."

I heard the collective sighs of relief from all three of them. "I'm directly to your left," Ellis said. "Can you focus on me?"

Turning, I blinked again and again to try and clear my vision. I used my eyelids like windshield wipers, trying to clear the blurriness in front of me. I saw something move. "What is that?" I asked.

"That's my hand moving in front of you. You saw it, which is a very good sign."

"Does that mean it worked?" I asked, afraid to believe it was real.

"I think it's safe to say it did. We'll need to wait a few weeks before we can establish what kind of vision you will have, but in the cases I have seen, you should return to the vision you had before the accident."

"Oh my goodness," I whispered, slowly moving my head and trying to see around the room. All I could see was shadows, but it seemed like my vision was clearing by the second. "Luke?"

"Over here," he said from my right.

I turned, desperately trying to see him. He looked like a giant blob. I saw movement and then felt his hand on my shoulder. Tears began to stream down my face as the reality of it all hit me. I was going to see again. I was suddenly overwhelmed with emotion. I was going to see again.

"Dad?"

"Right here," he said, identifying himself as the second blob.

"When will I see color?" I asked.

"I would imagine you will be seeing color by the end of the day. It will start with distinguishing between light and dark colors and with some time and retraining of your eyes and brain, you will see blacks and blues and so on."

I couldn't believe it. I was completely in awe. "Thank you," I said, through tears of joy. "Thank you so much."

"You are so welcome," Ellis answered. "Now, listen to me carefully, Bree. You have a couple difficult weeks ahead of you. I know it will be frustrating and you will want instant results, but you have to give your eyes some time. I will be sending you for follow-up care back in LA. We didn't see any damage to your retina, so I don't see any reason you won't have a full recovery."

I turned to look at Luke again. I was so desperate to see him. I knew I was staring and didn't care. "Okay. When can I go home?"

All three of them laughed before Ellis answered. "I need you to stay overnight for monitoring, and if everything looks okay, we'll get you out of here tomorrow morning."

"And I can fly tomorrow?"

"You can, but your father mentioned it might be best to stay one more night in Chicago and I happen to agree with him. You don't have any gas bubbles in your eye, but just in case there is a problem, I would like to have you close by."

"Okay, fine," I said, not even caring. I just wanted to see.

I felt something touch my hand. "These are those glasses I told you about. I'm going to leave a couple extra pairs. It is imperative that you wear them all the time. If you are home, in a dark room, you can take them off. If you are watching television, you need to wear them for the first week at least. Slowly, you can wear them less often. You are likely going to get headaches. That is brought on by eyestrain, and will be your signal that you've done too much and you need to rest your eyes."

"We'll make sure she gets plenty of rest," I heard Luke say.

I smiled. "Not too much rest," I replied. "I have a lot to make up for."

"Not all at once though," Ellis warned. "Take it slow. Little bits at a time. I would avoid reading a lot until your eyes are back to normal. Same with watching television or staring at a computer screen for more than fifteen minutes at a time. Think of your eyes as muscles. They need to be exercised and brought back to their previous strength."

"Okay," I nodded. "I will. I promise. I am never going to do anything to risk my eyesight again."

"I know you aren't going to want to hear this, but the nurse will be in this evening to cover your eyes again. It's just a precaution. We don't want you to accidentally injure your eyes while sleeping. Also, even though you don't have a bubble in your eye, I need you to lay face down for at least thirty minutes every hour."

I groaned. "No way."

"It's best for your recovery."

Despite how terrible it sounded, I was going to do anything I could to speed up my recovery. "Fine."

"I'll see you tomorrow," Ellis said, touching my arm. "I'm sure you're all exhausted, so try to get some sleep."

I saw a flash of light when she opened the door before we were plunged back into shadows. "Alright then, now what?"

My dad and Luke both laughed. "Take it easy," Luke said. "We've got all day."

"I want to see now," I said, slowly beginning to see a little more than just blobs. The shadows were becoming a little more defined. "I'm afraid it's all just a brief bit of sight."

"You heard what she said," my dad started. "You have to give your eyes time and don't strain them right out of the gate."

"I can see light, Dad. Do you know what that feels like? I don't feel like I'm trapped. I can quite literally see the light at the end of the tunnel. In my mind, I am racing towards that light and there is nothing that will stop me."

"I know," he said with a sigh. "That's what worries me. Just don't push too hard."

"I won't do anything that might cause damage, but for now, I want to bask in the light. I don't want to close my eyes. I want to look."

Chapter Two

Luke

I LOVED LOOKING INTO her eyes knowing that she could see me a little. Her eyes were gorgeous. Seeing them focused on me actually gave me chills. There was an intensity to her stare that made me feel like she was looking into my soul with those blue eyes. I knew it was her trying to focus, but it was a little intimidating.

"I need to make a call," Paul said. "I'll be back in a bit."

The moment he was gone, I took Bree's hand in mine. "How is it?" I asked her.

She took a deep breath. "I want to see your face so bad. I keep trying to force my eyes to clear but it's just so damn blurry."

"It's only been a few hours. She told you it would take some time."

"I know but I feel like I'm so close. I blink and squint thinking that will fix it and it doesn't."

"I have a feeling you are going to break the record when it comes to recovery. You are going to be looking at me in no time. For now, let's focus on the fact your sight is back. That is pretty damn amazing."

Her pretty smile warmed my heart. "It is. For so long, I was convinced it would never happen. I can't believe it's real. I won't believe it's real until I can actually see your face or read a magazine."

"Soon. What's the first thing you want to do when we get back home?"

She blew out her cheeks. "Everything. I have been thinking about the moment I could see again for almost three months. I don't know what I want to do first. I want to do everything."

I laughed, stroking my hand up and down her arm. It was good to see her happy. I was thrilled for her. "I think the beach is a good option. At sunset. I don't want to blind you. Literally."

She nodded. "That sounds beautiful, but how much will I be able to see?"

"I'm sure by the time we land back in California, you will already be seeing much clearer. The shadows will recede, and you will see outlines very soon."

"I'm going to hold you to that," she said.

I smiled and could no longer resist the urge to kiss her. I pressed my lips against her forehead, keeping it chaste—for now. "I can't wait until we can watch the sunset together."

Her hand reached up, touching my face before stroking over my head. "Me either. There is so much I want to do. I don't think I'm going to sleep for a week and it will have nothing to do with insomnia. It's going to be all about me wanting to see the world and do everything."

I stood up and brushed the hair away from her face. "I have a feeling you are going to be a real handful when we get home. I don't know if I'm going to be able to keep up with you."

"Do you think I'll be able to drive again?" she asked.

I laughed. "I think I would prefer you to be able to see more than shadow before you get behind the wheel."

She waved a hand. "You know what I mean. I don't think I lost my license. I never bothered to ask."

"We'll look into it when we get home," I told her.

The thought of her driving so soon after the surgery terrified me. She was a brave woman for wanting to try though. I knew a lot of people who were so afraid after a car accident, they couldn't even get in a car. I should have expected nothing less from her.

"Hello," a nurse said coming in the room. "Dr. Tanner said it was okay for you to try some broth. Are you feeling up to it?"

"Yes, actually, I am," Bree answered.

The nurse smiled at me. "I'll have a tray sent up shortly."

The door closed, leaving us alone once again. "Please tell me I can have something more than broth," she said.

I laughed. "As soon as you prove you can hold that broth down, they'll probably offer you something else. Now, you need to roll over."

"How awkward is it going to be to lay face down?" she complained.

"I'll get to check out your fine ass," I teased.

She smiled and gingerly rolled to her side. I moved her pillows out of the way and gave her the special pillow for her to lie on. We got her all situated just as Paul returned. "I've delayed the flight for another day," he announced.

"Why?" Bree mumbled from her awkward position.

"I've just spoken to Dr. Tanner," he started.

"I knew it!" Bree said, her voice muffled.

"She feels an extra day in Chicago near the hospital couldn't hurt. We covered the risks and I just think it makes sense to be close by in case one of those risks comes to life. You've come too far to have a complication set you back."

I slowly nodded and actually agreed with the man. I knew she was anxious to get home, but it was better to stay near just in case there was trouble. Plus, the flying was going to be more difficult than she realized. Ellis had gone over the recovery, but I knew Bree had just been focused on the end game. She had her eyes on the prize and all the other stuff didn't matter.

"I agree," I said. Paul looked at me and gave a slight nod.

"We'll enjoy the Chicago scene," he said, with forced enthusiasm. "We'll have a nice dinner and check out the sights."

"I can't—" Bree started to protest. "Oh shit," she breathed. "I can. Well, not actually see, but I will be able to see the lights, right?"

"Yes," I told her, happy to be along for the journey back to the land of the seeing with her. I wanted her to be happy and this was the first step in the right direction.

"I can't believe it," she said with obvious amazement. "I need to call Mel."

"I'll get your phone," I told her, moving to the small closet where her belongings had been stashed. I handed her the phone. "We'll give you a few minutes," I said, hoping her dad got the hint.

I had a feeling it was going to be a very emotional phone call and she deserved some privacy. Paul didn't look happy, but he followed me out of the room. We moved down the hall and into the small waiting room that was currently empty.

"You'll stay on for the next few weeks I presume," he said in a somewhat gruff tone.

I nodded. "I will stay as long as she needs me."

"And then you'll move out of the cottage?"

"Yes, of course." I was going to be homeless once again. A rolling stone. A man with no roots. "I'll start looking for a place as soon as we get back."

"And you two?" he asked.

I shrugged. "That's for her to decide."

Somehow, I got the distinct feeling that Paul was ready to push me out of Bree's life. I could go easy or he was going to put a boot in my ass and kick me out. I wasn't all that surprised. He was still upset with me over my little meltdown. I assured her I was fine, but I had shown weakness. Paul was not the kind of man who tolerated that.

"I agree," he said.

"I'll stay with her tonight," I volunteered.

He scowled at me. "I suppose that might be for the best. She might get anxious."

It was just after midnight when Ellis came in to check on Bree. I was half asleep in the recliner the noc-shift nurse brought me. Bree wasn't happy to have the bandages put back on. I had taken over the job from the nurse, which seemed to make it a little easier for Bree to handle. She was restless. The on-call doctor had prescribed a mild sedative to help her sleep.

"How is she?" Ellis whispered.

"Good. Really good. I can't believe it worked."

She softly laughed. "Thanks for the confidence."

"I'm sorry, but there's a reason it's still considered experimental. I had faith in you, but I'm not sure I had faith it would work. It just seemed too easy."

She checked the screen that gave her a quick peek at Bree's vitals. "It is easy. It's a shame it isn't done more often. I hope with Bree's success, it will become one."

"Do you think her vision will be totally restored?" I asked, knowing she had answered the same question before, but I wanted to hear her say it to me.

She nodded. "I do. I think Bree is going to go on to have a normal, happy life. You two are good together. I can see how much you both care for each other. I'm happy for you."

"Thanks. I hope it works out."

She raised an eyebrow. "You don't think it will?"

"I think there are some people who would prefer it didn't."

She smiled. "The overprotective daddy, I assume?"

"Yes."

"You're a good guy, Luke. He'll see that soon enough. If not, from the very little time I have spent with Bree, I don't think it will matter. She's a fighter. If she wants you, she's going to have you."

I grinned. "I am all hers to have."

"I can see that. Try and get some sleep. I'll do rounds around ten tomorrow and discharge her then."

"Thank you. Truly, you've done something amazing here."

"You are welcome and so is Bree. This was my pleasure and you better believe I will be writing an article on it."

"You deserve the credit," I told her.

She smiled and walked out. I checked to make sure Bree was asleep. Her heart rate was nice and steady, and the deep sounds of her breathing made me smile. She was at peace. Tomorrow was going to be a busy day. We were staying in the city, but I knew Bree and she was going to be like a kid lose in a candy store. She was going to give her eyes one hell of a workout.

I just hoped we could keep up with her. I considered asking for a few extra tranquilizers to try and keep her calm for the first few days but knew it would be futile. She was going to do what she had been craving for too long. She was going to be a free woman.

Chapter Three

Bree

WE WERE HOME. MY TEMPORARY home. I was already planning on looking for my own place. I was not going to live with my father for the rest of my days. My sight was getting better by the hour. Everything was still extremely blurry, but I was able to distinguish between people and things.

"I'm sorry," Luke said, when his hand went to my elbow. "Old habits."

I laughed. "It's okay. I sometimes forget I'm supposed to be using my eyes at all. I'm so used to using my foot as a walking stick."

"I'll get the door," my father said.

I heard the door open and realized I wasn't just hearing it. I saw it as well. My brain was still trying to relearn how to use my eyes. It was crazy to see again. I walked inside the mansion, the familiar scent of wood polish and lemon cleaner welcomed me. It was oddly comforting to be back in the place that had served as my prison for months.

"I want to go out back," I said.

"Keep your sunglasses on," my father warned.

I rolled my eyes, something that somehow seem more satisfying now. "I know, Dad."

The giant, dark glasses had been a fixture on my face for the last two days. I didn't mind them too much. The sun had been awfully bright when we landed in California. I could already feel a headache coming on, but I wasn't going to tell Luke or my dad. They would have me tucked in bed with the curtains drawn and the lights off.

"I'll go with her," Luke said.

"I'm going to make some calls," my dad said and left us alone.

Luke and I walked outside and I stopped to take it all in. "The pool," I breathed, seeing the general outline of the pool and the lounge chairs dotted around the edge.

"Can you see the pool, or you just know where it is?"

"I can see it. I can't see the water that I know is crystal clear, but I can see it."

"Do you want to sit down?" he asked.

I turned to look at him. I couldn't see him clearly, but I had a general idea of what he looked like. I was desperate to look into his eyes, but the more I tried to focus on his eyes, the blurrier my vision got, and I ended up going cross-eyed. I had to give it time. At least that is what I had been told a million times.

"I would like that."

Despite the fact I could see the chair, Luke still guided me. I had a feeling it was more about who he was as a gentleman than about him trying to help me. "I'll keep you company until Mel shows up. She texted saying she would be right over."

"I can't wait to see her," I said with excitement. "Like actually see her. I know my world was only dark for a few months, but it felt like an eternity. I truly want to see everything. I want to do everything. It is going to be so hard to sleep the next few days. I'm not great at waiting. I want to do everything now."

"I can only imagine. I'm happy for you. I'm happy to take you anywhere you want to go. I don't think anyone is quite ready to hand you the keys to a car yet."

I laughed. "That is going to be one of the first things I do when I can see completely. That, and finding my own place. We can start doing that right away."

"Have you talked to your father about that?"

"No, but I will. It was always made very clear I've been planning to get my own place whether the surgery was a possibility or not. Me living in this house was always temporary. I can't live with my dad."

"I get it," he answered.

I felt like Luke was a little more reserved than usual and I wasn't sure what was going on. With my father constantly around, he and I had not had the chance to really talk. Now wasn't the right time either. Mel would be there soon, and we never knew when my father was going to pop up. It was just another reason I needed my own place. I felt like I was being watched at every turn.

"Two weeks," I said.

"What's in two weeks?" he asked.

I realized I had been thinking out loud. "The follow-up with Ellis. She said she has to check for cataract development and if it isn't there, I am in the clear. Two weeks. It feels like a lifetime."

"You've come a long way in a short time," he answered. "Every day your vision is getting better. I have no doubt in my mind you are going to be fine."

I studied his profile. I could see the general outline of his face and every chance I got, I stared at him. I was committing every little detail to memory. I knew there was a chance that cataracts could develop, and I could be back to being blind in a matter of months. Cataracts would mean another surgery. I just wanted my eyes to work.

Hearing a scream, I immediately knew Mel had arrived. Poor Luke jumped out of his chair so fast I worried he would fall headfirst in the pool. "Holy shit," he growled. "Why in the hell is she screaming?"

I got up from my chair and waited. I could see Mel's figure racing towards me. A second later, she had her arms around me, hugging me so tight I couldn't breathe. When she finally released me, we both stared at each other for a long time. It was easier to see her because I knew what she looked like. My brain filled in the blanks my blurry vision left.

"I'm going to leave you two alone," Luke said. "I'll be in the cottage if you need me."

"Bye, thank you," I said again. I had been saying thank you a lot in the last couple days. I felt like I owed him and my dad and Ellis and the rest of the team of doctors a great deal of thanks. I owed them my life.

"Oh my gosh, look at you," Mel exclaimed.

"I see me," I grinned. "Kind of."

"You are really rocking the hell out of those shades," she teased.

I giggled. "I was thinking we could bedazzle them or something."

"How long do you have to wear them?"

"At least a couple weeks."

"I can't believe you can see me," she said, and I heard the emotion in her voice.

I gave her another hug. "Me either. It is truly a miracle. I feel like I have been given a second chance at life. I don't want to waste a single minute."

"I know you, and I know you aren't going to be able to sit still."

We both sat down again. It was so nice to be able to see the person I was talking to. "I want to start looking for a place right away. Luke is going to talk to my dad and find out where all my art supplies were stashed. I want to paint. Maybe I can do abstract for a while until I get my vision back. I have a feeling no matter what I try to paint, it's going to look abstract anyway."

She laughed. "Not for you. You truly could make a beautiful picture with your eyes closed."

"I doubt it."

"So, have you *seen* Luke? What do you think? He's hot, right?"

I smiled. "I've got a better idea about what he looks like, but honestly, I wouldn't care if he was an ogre. It's strange to know someone so well and be in love with them without seeing them."

"I think that's called internet dating," she quipped.

I laughed. "I suppose in a way it is like that. We got to know each other so well. It's like I have an image of him in my mind based on what I know about him."

"But can you see him?" she asked.

I smiled, slowly nodding. "Mostly and I am very happy."

"Does that mean you guys are officially a thing again? You two go up and down more than a rollercoaster."

I shrugged. "I don't think it's official just yet. We've barely had time to talk."

"Do you think he'll stick around?"

I let out a long sigh. "I know he is going to start looking for a job."

"Because you don't need him anymore?"

"Yes, basically. It will be a couple weeks, maybe longer before I can really see again. Then of course, there is always the chance this might be as good as it gets."

"Don't start thinking like that again," she warned.

"I'm trying to stay positive, but it is in the back of my mind. Ellis told me a few of the patients that got the surgery only got minimal vision back. She said those patients had other damage to the retina or something, but I can't help but wonder if I'm going to be one of those."

"It's early. Don't start borrowing trouble just yet. Give your body a chance to heal. The fact you can see at all is a miracle."

I nodded. "I agree. I totally agree. There is so much I want to do and I'm afraid to dream too much, just in case."

"Hey, you didn't want to think about the surgery working at all and it did. Dream big. Start thinking about what you want to do with your life."

I grinned. "I am. I can't help but think about much of anything else. I'm thinking about looking for a house instead of an apartment this time."

"What? Really?"

I shrugged. "I want to put down roots. I want to have a stable home—just in case."

"Just in case what?"

I turned to look at her. "Just in case my vision is only temporary. It's weird, but I'm kind of okay with that. I am going to thank my lucky stars every minute I have my sight, but if it fades or doesn't get any better than what it is, I'm going to accept it. I'm not going to fight and scream and let myself sink into a deep depression."

"I get that, but don't go down for the count just yet."

I smiled and turned my face up to the sun. I closed my eyes. The sun was still crazy bright, even with the dark lenses shielding my eyes. It felt so good to actually see the sun. "I'm not. You better believe I'm going to fight like hell to keep these eyes working."

"Good girl. When are we going shopping?"

I laughed. "I'm not sure I'm going to be much good just yet."

"Soon. The moment you do, we are going to take an entire weekend and do some serious shopping."

"I'll tell my dad to dust off my cards," I said with a grin.

"I have a feeling he is going to be more than happy to let you have a shopping spree. I talked to him for a minute when I got here. He is elated."

"I know. It was really hard on him. It's another reason I need to move out. We had a great relationship before the accident. Things have been a little strained between us and I want to get back to the way things were."

"And you want to be alone with your hunky nurse," she teased.

I had to laugh. "Maybe that too."

"He's a good one," she said. "Don't let him get away."

"Trust me, I don't plan on it."

I was already planning my future with Luke. I knew he was planning on moving out of the cottage. I had overheard him and my father talking that first night in the hospital. It was going to take my dad some time to get used to the idea of me and Luke together. That was fine. I was hoping to find a house that Luke and I could share. Yes, I was totally getting ahead of myself. I couldn't help it. I wanted to live. I wanted to live as much as I could just in case my second chance at life was cut short.

I wanted to be happy with a man and play house. I wanted to do all the things I thought I was never going to get to do. I had the chance and I planned on using every minute I had left on this earth to make myself happy.

Chapter Four

Luke

I WOKE EARLY TO THE sound of my phone ringing. I reached out, pulled it to my face and without opening my eyes, answered it. "Hello?" I muttered, none too thrilled to be pulled out of a very nice dream about Bree.

"Luke?" my mother's strained voice dame through the phone.

I inwardly groaned. "Yes, Mom?"

"Luke, is that you?"

High drama. I expected nothing less from the woman. "Yes, Mom. You called me. What's up?"

"I'm sick. Something is terribly wrong. I think my kidneys are shutting down."

I sighed. "Why do you think that?"

"Oh, I am in so much pain and I'm so sick. My kidneys hurt."

I shook my head, wishing like hell I could just have a normal mother. "Take some ibuprofen and drink some cranberry juice."

"This is different. Luke, I need you."

I sighed, throwing off the blanket and sitting on the edge of the bed in nothing but my briefs. "Mom, you don't need me. I just told you what to do."

"And how am I supposed to get cranberry juice?" she snapped. "I can't hardly move."

"Call a delivery service," I answered.

"Luke, I can't afford that! I can't believe you are truly going to leave me alone to die."

I rubbed a hand over my head, trying to wake myself up. "Call the doctor. Call an ambulance. Go to the hospital if you think it's that serious. I'm not going to fly to Texas to get you cranberry juice."

I heard her gasp. "What is wrong with you! How dare you treat me so terribly. I'm your mother!"

"Yes, you are, and I am telling you that if you are sick, go to the doctor. I can't help you. I'm in California and I have a job."

She made a hissing sound. "A job. I didn't know shacking up with your girlfriend was considered work these days."

She was in one of her nasty moods. If I was back home in Texas, I would be stuck listening to her insults. I wasn't in Texas. I didn't have to take her verbal abuse until she got what she wanted—my attention. "I'm going to go now."

"Don't hang up!" she wailed. "I need you. Let's stop this nonsense. You just need to come home."

"I'm not coming home. Goodbye, Mother."

I ended the call and tossed the phone on my bed. Letting out a long sigh, I rubbed both hands down my face to try and erase the feeling of dread I always got when she was in one of her moods. I was so glad I lived too far away for her to pop up unannounced. Even though she had done that once already, I was sure she couldn't afford another plane ticket to California.

There was no way I was leaving Bree. Not now. Not when things were going so well between us. I knew we were headed for some serious changes, but I was ready for it. We had yet to talk about what we were going to be, but I was confident things would be good between us. I felt such a strong pull to her, and I loved seeing her happy. It made my heart swell to see her smiling so brightly all the time.

Paul was going to be at work today which meant Bree and I could finally be alone. The man had been hovering a lot. I wasn't sure what his deal was, but I had a feeling he wanted to push me out. I was fine as the hired help, but he didn't want me to be romantically involved with his daughter. He was a nice enough man and I knew he that he was looking out for Bree, but I would never hurt her.

I headed for the shower, anxious to get over to the main house and see Bree. I wasn't sure what she wanted to do today, but I was sure she was already up and chomping at the bit to get a move on with something. She had been moving at a hundred miles an hour since those bandages had come off.

Dressing quickly, I reminded myself to pay a little more attention to what I wore. Now that she could see me, I wanted to impress her a bit. She was a gorgeous woman and I wanted her to want me as much as I wanted her. Truthfully, there had been a little part of me that was worried she wouldn't find me attractive. I knew her well enough to know she wouldn't be the type to kick me to the curb because I didn't measure up, but I didn't want her eye to wander now that she could see.

I headed over to the house, hoping like hell Paul was already gone. I stopped walking when I spotted Bree sitting on the patio. She had on those giant sunglasses that made her look ridiculous, but in the cutest way possible. I knew the moment she saw me. A huge smile spread over her face and she waved. It was still strange getting used to the idea of her actually seeing me.

"Good morning," I said, as I started walking towards her.

She got to her feet, showing off those long, beautiful legs clad in a pair of jean shorts with little frayed edges hanging over her tanned thighs. She was wearing a pretty pink sweater that hung off her shoulders. Her hair was brushed to a shine and looked like she had taken some time to style it. "Good morning. I made you coffee."

I watched as she reached for the cup with purpose. Gone were the tentative, slow movements she used when she was feeling things out.

She could see. I had to keep reminding myself—she could see. "You look stunning this morning."

"Thank you. You look very handsome." She burst into giggles. "I can't believe I can say you look about anything. You look. Seriously! I can see!"

"How is it this morning?" I asked, taking the offered coffee.

She nodded. "Good. It's always much clearer in the morning, and then by this afternoon it will be blurry. Let me look at you."

I stood perfectly still while she stepped towards me. Her hand touched my cheek. She smiled as she trailed her fingers over my jaw. It was slightly awkward to be studied with such intensity, but I understood she had to be close to truly see. I didn't mind that it was her. It was very intimate.

"Is your Dad here?" I asked on a breath.

Her hand dropped away. "Nope. He left about twenty minutes ago. I have a little surprise for you."

I liked the sound of that. "A surprise?"

Her soft laughter floated around me. "Yes, but not that. He told me all my stuff is upstairs in my old room."

"The art stuff?" I asked. She had talked about tracking it down. I was glad to know it was close.

"Yep. I was hoping you could help me dig it out and grab my paints and stuff. Then maybe a trip to the art supply store so I can pick up some new canvases."

I smiled, thrilled to see her getting right back into the groove of things. "Absolutely."

"I can make you breakfast first," she offered.

"I'm good. When we go out, we can grab something to eat if you're up for it."

"That works for me."

"How are you feeling, though, in general I mean?" I usually looked at her eyes and her face to get an idea of how she slept. The giant shades made that impossible. "Did you sleep okay?"

She shrugged. "I was restless, but only because I'm anxious to find my art stuff."

"Then we should probably go on a treasure hunt."

She led me upstairs, a place I had never been in all the time I had been working for them. There was never a need to go upstairs. It was just as luxurious as the ground floor. "This is my old room," she said, stopping in front of a pair of double doors.

She pushed the door open and I was immediately impressed. There was a huge four-poster bed with a pink comforter. All around the room there were pictures of butterflies and woodland scenes. The room was huge. There was a dark blue chaise lounge positioned near the huge bank of windows that lined one wall. I could imagine her sitting there and reading.

To the left there was a door which I assumed was the adjoining bathroom. She walked towards it and opened the door to reveal a closet. "Holy shit," I said with genuine shock. "That's your closet?"

She laughed. "I'm not going to say I wasn't spoiled."

The clothes had been cleaned out and in their place were totes and boxes with her name on them. I was assuming it was her art supplies. "Did your dad put the rest of your stuff in storage?" I questioned. "You said you had your own place."

She nodded. "Yes. The bulk of my clothes were moved into the room downstairs, but my furniture was put into storage."

"Why didn't you keep the apartment?"

"There didn't seem to be any point. I wasn't convinced I would ever see again, and it was on the eighth floor of the building. I figured if I ever did move out, I would need something I could adapt to my situation."

My eyes scanned the area, landing on a stack of canvases leaning up against the back wall. I walked to them and pulled one forward, finding a picture on the other side. I picked up the large sixteen by twenty canvas and stared at the painting of our spot at the beach. It was a sunset view, complete with warm orange and red hues streaking across the sky. In the bottom of the frame there was a young woman with a straw hat sitting on the beach.

"This is beautiful," I said. "Did you paint this?"

I walked closer to her, holding up the picture. She wrinkled her nose. "I did. That was a couple years ago. It isn't one of my best."

"Bree, this is gorgeous. I love it. Who is the woman in the picture?"

She shrugged. "I don't know. She was at the beach, just sitting there. At first I didn't intend to put her in the picture and then I just kind of roughed her in."

I nodded. "I'm impressed. Truly. When you told me you liked art, I didn't realize just how talented you are."

"I dabble. I'm not nearly as good as some of the other local artists."

"If this is dabbling, I can't imagine what you can do when you actually try."

I walked back to the stack of canvases and pulled each one out, turning them around and marveling at her true talent. The majority of the paintings were of the beach and other outdoor scenes. It was her life. Her paintings said so much about her.

"I want to buy a house and put in an art studio. I want to paint. I crave painting. I have all these images in my head that I want to put on canvas."

"Where do you want to set up for now?" I asked, anxious to help her.

"In here is fine. I used to love painting in front of the windows."

"Alright, let's do this."

We spent the rest of the day unpacking her art supplies and getting her easels set up. The extra light from the windows allowed her to see better than anywhere else in the room. Then after a quick trip into town, she had an art studio ready to go. When I left for the day, I was looking forward to a future with her. Seeing her art and watching her face light up when she picked out new brushes showed me a side of her I had never seen before.

She was beautiful in every way.

Chapter Five

Bree

I HAD TRIED, REALLY tried to sleep in, but I couldn't do it. I needed to paint. While I couldn't make out a lot of the details, I wanted to feel the brush in my hand. I wanted to feel it sweeping across the canvas. I wanted to see color. I had taken a few classes that focused on abstract paintings. That is what I was telling myself I was doing. I could see general colors and if I took off the glasses, I could get a better idea about the shades.

Still, I never left the glasses off for long. I was being very careful with my recovery. I wasn't going to risk losing my sight again. My father had ordered a ridiculously bright LED shop light for me to use when I lost the bright light of day. I was in a bit of a pickle with the lighting issue. Bright lights allowed me to see with the dark sunglasses on that dulled the colors. No lights meant I didn't need to wear the glasses but then I couldn't see.

Also, I found myself clinging to the light. I didn't want to be in the darkness ever again. Never. I had a blue nightlight that was soft on my eyes, but I couldn't leave it on all night. I couldn't wait until I was normal again. I couldn't wait until I could go outside and really enjoy the sun.

"Soon," I told myself, picking up the wide brush and dipping it in the royal blue paint.

Letting myself fall into a peaceful rhythm, it just felt good to be doing what I loved. I had been dreaming about the gallery idea, and now that I knew what I wanted, I was going after it. Before the accident, it was one of those things I thought a lot about, but never put a lot of effort into making it happen. I was going to now.

Hearing a knock on my door, I assumed it was Luke. "Come in," I called out.

I turned and immediately knew it wasn't him. I tilted my head to the side, focusing my eyes on the face. "Nate?"

"You can see me!"

I smiled. "Mostly. You're still a little blurry."

"I spoke with your father. He said you were back, and that the surgery worked. I wanted to come by and say hi."

Though we were a disaster together, I didn't hate Nate. I no longer blamed him for the accident either. It had been an accident and I was the only one that deserved any blame. Putting down my brush, I wiped my hands on the smock I was wearing. "Thank you."

He walked towards me and pulled me in for a hug. I hugged him back, genuinely happy we could still be friends. "It's good to see you painting again."

"It feels good to be doing it."

"Abstract?" he asked.

I laughed. "I can't quite see fine lines just yet, but I couldn't wait to start painting."

"It will be great."

"Come have a seat and tell me what you have been up to the last few months," I said, as I walked towards the cozy seating area.

"Well, for starters, your father gave me a job," he announced.

"He did?" I said, blinking several times.

"I thought he would have told you."

"No, he didn't," I said, shaking my head. I found it a little odd but wondered if the reason he hadn't hired Nate before was because we were dating. Maybe he wanted to keep his two worlds separate.

"Does that bother you?" Nate asked.

"No, not at all. I'm happy for you. Are you designing software?"

He chuckled. "No. Your dad has an army of young kids doing that. I'm overseeing the software production and basically keeping the kids in order."

"I doubt you're much older than they are," I said with a laugh.

"Well, I feel like I'm a hundred years older than they are. So, what's next for you? I know you and assume you're already planning something big."

"First, I'm going to finish letting my eyes get back to normal," I said with a grin. Then, I'm going to start looking for a house and a space for an art gallery. Then, I'm going to start traveling like I always wanted to and curate a collection for my gallery."

He burst into laughter. "Gee, that's all?"

I smiled. "I told you before I wanted to open a gallery. I always thought I had time and I could put it off. I don't want to put it off anymore. I want to do it. I've spent the last three months thinking about what I didn't do. Now that I have a chance, I'm going to get busy and do all those things I regretted not doing."

"You have a new lease on life," he replied.

I nodded. "I do and it is amazing. I know as soon as I get these glasses off, everything is going to be more vivid. More exciting. I want to look at everything and commit it to memory, just in case I lose my sight again."

"Is that a possibility?" he asked, with real concern.

"It is. Ellis, Dr. Tanner, doesn't think it will happen, but there is a chance I could need another surgery down the road. The bottom line is that I don't take my sight for granted and I want to enjoy it while I have it."

"I think that sounds like a very good plan." He was quiet for a few seconds. I knew him well enough to know he had something more to say. I waited, giving him time to collect his thoughts.

"Bree, I'm so sorry about that night. I have replayed that fight about a million times and keep thinking about what I could have said or that I should have done to stop you from leaving."

"I was stubborn. I would have left regardless. It isn't your fault."

"I feel terrible about it," he said.

I reached out, taking his hand in mine. I hated that he felt guilty, and while I had been angry with him for a long time, I knew it wasn't his fault.

"It's over. It wasn't your fault. It was an accident. I'm moving on with my life and you should too."

"I know what you said that night, but I need to know, were you serious? Did you, do you really want to break up?"

I bit my lower lip. "Yes, I do. I know you didn't get much of a chance to give your opinion on the matter and I'm sorry for that, but this is for the best. You've got a great job now and I want to do things I know you don't necessarily approve of. I hope we can still be friends."

"Absolutely. I do care about you and I only want the best for you."

He squeezed my hand. It was a familiar feeling. We had spent a lot of time together and while I knew I didn't love him, I did still care about him as a friend. "Thank you."

"I didn't know you had company," Luke's voice cut through the air like a sharp blade.

I whipped my head around, staring at the blurry image of him. I couldn't see the look on his face, but I heard the tone of his voice. "Hi," I said with a smile.

"I'll come back later," he mumbled, turning to leave.

"I was just leaving," Nate said, giving my hand a last squeeze before getting up.

"Thank you for coming by," I said standing up as well.

"I'll talk to you soon," Nate said, and walked out.

Luke was still standing near the door. "I didn't know you two were seeing each other again."

"Oh please," I said, putting a hand on my hip. "We aren't seeing each other. He came by to check on me."

I heard him scoff. "Looked like you two were pretty friendly."

"Luke, we are friends. He was my boyfriend for three years. I want to be friends with him."

"So, I saw."

"Don't do that," I snapped. "Don't get jealous about me talking to Nate. He is my friend."

"Do you hold hands with all your friends?" he growled.

"Not that it is really any of your business, but I was offering him comfort. He was feeling guilty about the fight we had and the accident. I was letting him know it was okay."

"None of my business," he repeated. "I see."

I was not going to deal with an overly possessive man, especially considering we weren't officially together. He was the one who ended things and had made no move to start things up. I wasn't sure that was what he wanted.

"You're the one who said we were keeping things professional. As my professional caregiver, I really don't think you get to have an opinion about my personal life."

"Bree, you know why I said that," he argued.

"I do, and that's where we are."

"Good to know."

"Luke, please stop this. I don't want to fight with you. I'm in a great place right now and a lot of that is because of you. Can we just be happy together? I know I still some recovery in front of me. I'm ready to do that and I am hoping you will continue to help me. Is that what you want?"

He was quiet for too long. "Yes," he finally answered. "But I don't like him."

"I'm sorry, but Nate isn't a bad guy. I don't love him, but he is my friend."

"Does that mean he's going to be coming around more often?"

I shrugged. "I don't know. I don't expect it will be a regular thing, but I'm sure I will see him now and again, especially considering he apparently works at my father's company now."

"What?" Luke gasped.

"Yes, apparently my dad hired him, which is weird because he never would when we were together."

"I see," he said in a tight voice. He cleared his throat. "Have you had your breakfast yet?"

The way he said it was all very professional. I could tell he was still upset about seeing Nate. One of these days, he and I were going to have to decide what we were doing. I loved him and I was sure he loved me, but if he was one of those crazy jealous types, it would never work. I had a lot of life to live and I wasn't going to be held back by a jealous boyfriend. I had already been there and done that.

"I haven't," I answered. "I got up early and came up to paint."

"I'll make you something," he said, stepping out of the room.

"You don't need to do that."

"I'm your caregiver still. I do need to do it and I would like to."

I sighed and followed him out of the room. "Thank you."

"Is there anything you want to do today?" he asked, as we walked downstairs together.

"There are about a million things I would like to do, but I think I'll have to wait a couple more weeks before I can."

"Like?" he asked.

"Like start looking at properties, and visiting a couple art galleries. I'll wait until I can see better for that. Today, I would like to paint."

"Okay, then today will be all about painting. We could move one of those easels into the garden like you talked about."

"I would love that. Gosh, I can't until I can take these damn glasses off. It's like wearing a filter all the time."

"Another two weeks or so and you should be good to go in the house. Though she did say being outside might take a little longer."

I groaned. "Too long."

Chapter Six

Luke

THERE WAS SOME SERIOUS tension between us, and it was my fault. I had come in hot when I walked in on her and Nate. I didn't like what I saw, but like she said, it was none of my fucking business. I watched her paint from my spot in the chair Nate had been sitting in. There was something soothing about watching her work.

"What do you think?" she turned to ask me.

I smiled. "I think you are a real artist. I feel like I am watching Bob Ross."

She laughed. "Is that boring?"

"Not at all," I assured her. "Do you have the vision in your mind when you start?"

She shrugged and dipped paintbrush in the solvent. "Usually, yes, but without being able to truly see, I'm just kind of painting with colors. Does that make sense?"

I looked at the swirls of pastel colors with an obvious butterfly in blue. "I think so. I see a butterfly."

She grinned. "Yes. Very good."

"It's pretty. I like your other work with the scenes, but this feels like one of those pictures that you stare at and just kind of lose focus."

"Thank you. These paintings are not going in a gallery and will likely end up in the trash. I'm just enjoying having a brush in my hand."

"I get it. It's good to warm up before you create a masterpiece any-way. Do you have something in mind? Once your sight is clear?"

She looked thoughtful. "I'm not sure yet. Usually, I have to be in-spired. Without really, truly seeing anything, I'm not feeling very in-spired."

"Hello!" Paul's voice boomed down the hall.

I checked my watch and realized it was already six o'clock. It seemed I'd gotten completely lost in the just watching her paint. "I guess that's my cue."

"You don't have to run off when he gets here," she said, taking off her smock.

"You guys need your time together. I'll see you tomorrow."

She was staring at me, and I always wondered just how much she could see. She would tilt her head from left to right like she was sizing me up. "I'll probably be up here."

"Then I will see you here," I said, tempted to kiss her but walking away instead.

Paul stopped me in the hall. "How is she?" he asked.

"Good. Really good. She's in good spirits and seems to be getting better every day."

He smiled and nodded. "Good. I knew that surgery was the right thing to do."

"It was a risk, but definitely worth it."

He was looking at me strangely. "You've done well with her."

"Thank you," I said. "I'll go. I'll be back in the morning."

He nodded and walked by without saying another word. I headed outside and made my way to the cottage. I knew my days on the prop-erty were numbered. Bree wasn't planning on staying for much longer either. She had said she wanted to start looking for property soon. I had no idea if she was wealthy herself or if it was going to be her dad buy-ing her the house and I was interested in seeing what she would want, a mansion or something more modest.

When I got to the cottage, I let myself think about what I had witnessed between her and Nate. It was still eating at me. I couldn't help but notice the way Nate looked at her. He loved her and wanted her back. It was obvious. She might believe they were just friends, but I saw something more. He had several advantages over me. The biggest being Paul. I got the feeling Paul wanted her with Nate. The guy didn't just stop by. Paul had hired him and now they were all buddy-buddy. I had a feeling Paul encouraged the visit and that did not bode well for me.

Grabbing a beer from the fridge, I sat down, looking around the cottage. This cottage, a house that was essentially an extra for the Sullivan family, was nicer than anything I could ever afford. It was a stark reminder of the differences between me and Bree. I was a nobody from Texas, with no chance of ever being someone like Nate. Not that I wanted to be the suit and tie, kiss ass fop that he was, but he was the kind of guy that was meant to be wealthy. He was the kind of guy that knew what fork to use at dinner.

Me? I was the guy sitting on a borrowed couch, in a borrowed house drinking a beer straight from the bottle. I didn't have connections to the rich and powerful. I didn't know her social circle. Nate had it all. He had been a part of her life for years. And Paul liked him.

That was the kicker. It hurt that Paul didn't think I was good enough for his daughter. I had done nothing to make him think I was some loser from the wrong side of the tracks, but he still didn't want me with her. I could feel it coming off him in waves. He wanted more for her. A nurse with no future job prospects was not going to be good enough for him.

Bree was different. She wasn't about money and prestige. She was humble and kind and we got along very well. At least, she had been that way. Maybe now that she had her sight back, she would be a different person. I got to know the Bree that timms frightened and insecure. She had depended on me. She had been the one worried about me looking elsewhere for romance.

"Oh, how the tables have turned," I mumbled into my beer.

I wasn't that guy, I told myself. I wasn't that guy that got jealous or felt insecure. I was more laid back. At least, I thought I was. I didn't have a lot of experience with girlfriends. Usually, I would casually date someone before I figured out it wasn't going to work. Or, they would realize my mother occupied the majority of my time and they would just kind of fade out of my life.

But I'd never really cared before now. I didn't want to lose Bree. I loved her. I wanted to be with her more than I had ever wanted to be with another woman. She was beautiful, inside and out. I wanted to be with her as she took the first steps into her new life. I wanted to watch her blossom. The butterfly she had painted was a representation of herself. She was changing and coming out of her cocoon as an even more beautiful person.

Finished with my beer, I took the bottle back to the kitchen. I couldn't believe I was acting like a whiny bitch. Bree wasn't mine to be jealous of. I wanted her to have the time to find that independence she was craving. I was willing to wait in the shadows while she found herself. But I wasn't willing to wait while Nate swooped in. Where had he been the last couple months when she was in her darkest hour? Where had he been when she was scared and hurting?

Though I also knew she wasn't mine to claim. I couldn't just decide I was the man for her. That had to come from her. I had watched her stare at me for long minutes. I always held still, letting her look her as long as she wanted. I knew her eyes were still adjusting, and she was trying to focus on my face. I walked into the bathroom and looked at my reflection. What was she seeing when she looked at me?

Nate and I were very different. Nate's dark hair versus my light hair. My light eyes versus his dark eyes. He was an average guy, more of a tennis player build. He wore slacks and button-up shirts and had that Wall Street look about him. She had been with the man for three years. Was that really what she was attracted to?

I was not a Nate. I had the look of a workhorse. I had the look of a man born to do manual labor. It was what had landed me so many modeling jobs in my younger years. I couldn't count the number of times I had been posed in nothing but a pair of jeans and a cowboy hat with straw almost always involved.

Blue-collar. Nate was white-collar. We were two guys on opposite ends of the spectrum, with Bree right in the middle. I wasn't foolish enough to believe Nate stopped by to check on her as a friend. He knew she had her sight back and he was planning on swooping in and picking up where they left off.

I didn't believe Bree was that naïve, either. She had to know what Nate was doing. The guy had been nothing more than a ghost the last couple of months and now he was suddenly back and wanting to be friends. I was calling bullshit. He was back, with Paul's blessing.

Still, I wished I was more confident. I wished I could say without a doubt that Bree wanted to be with me. I couldn't say that at this point. I wasn't sure I was the man she wanted. She was used to fancy things and nice restaurants. I couldn't give her any of that. She would be the one with all the money and in my opinion, the power. I wasn't man enough to surrender myself to her. I needed to feel useful. I needed to be needed.

With her sight back, she didn't need me. I would always be her plus one. I would always be the guy she had to introduce because no one knew me or would have heard about me. I wasn't a mover and shaker in the IT world or any world for that matter. If I didn't find a job soon, I was going to be homeless.

"And back home to Mommy," I muttered, curling my lip in disgust at the very thought.

"Fuck that," I said, shaking my head.

I was not going back home. No way. I would take a job in another city before I did that. I would take one of those traveling nurse jobs. I wasn't going back home. I would find a way to stick around for a while.

I needed to give Bree some time to make up her mind. I reminded myself it had been less than a week since the surgery. She needed time to work on herself before she could make any decisions about a relationship.

Hopefully, Nate would give her the space she needed to make that decision. I was terrified she would go back to the life she knew. The life she was familiar with. She said she broke up with Nate, but they had been together three years. That wasn't the kind of relationship that ended with a fight over Chinese food.

So, I needed to prepare myself for the worst. Bree was a woman who deserved the best. Maybe I wasn't the best choice for her. I knew Nate wasn't, but he could give her things I never could.

Chapter Seven

Bree

I WALKED DOWNSTAIRS with my hand firmly on the rail. My depth perception was a little skewed. When I saw Ellis, I planned on asking her if that was going to be my new normal. I could work around it and was definitely grateful for the progress I did have, but I needed to prepare myself.

Stepping onto the hard floor, I took a second to orientate myself and followed my nose to the dining room. The cook had prepared something that smelled amazing. My father had used the intercom system to let me know dinner was ready. I was looking forward to having dinner with him. He had been really busy as of late, and I felt like we rarely talked anymore.

"There you are," he said, getting to his feet.

"I wanted to finish up," I told him.

He stepped towards me and gave me a quick hug before pulling my chair out for me. He loved to practice his good manners, even when it was just the two of us. I felt a little underdressed for what was obviously a nice dinner.

"How is it going up there?" he asked.

"Good," I answered with a smile. "I'm getting back into the swing of things."

"That's excellent," he answered.

I wasn't sure if he was all that thrilled with my painting again. He had always supported it as a hobby, but nothing more. He wanted me to work in the company with him. He wanted me to run the company one day. But I did not love technology, in fact, my brain just didn't grasp it the way some people could. I was not the kind of woman who could be in an office day in and day out. I couldn't sit in board meetings and plot ways to become even wealthier.

While I appreciated the wealth he earned from his company, it just wasn't my path in life. I needed something different. "I'm still thinking about opening an art gallery," I said, floating the idea once again.

He made a grunting sound. "That's good."

He was placating me, but I didn't mind. "I cannot wait to go to Mastro's. Now that I can see the food on my plate, I won't make an ass of myself."

He chuckled. "You could never do that dear."

"Yes, I could. As soon as things get a little clearer, I'm making a reservation."

"You just let me know and it will be my treat," he offered.

"Thanks, Dad. Soon. Keep your calendar open."

He laughed. "I will do that for you."

"Is Nate working out well for you?" I asked, hoping to broach the subject once again. When he had come into the room earlier, he didn't seem to want to talk about it. He claimed he had phone calls to make, but I wasn't letting him off the hook that easily.

"He is," he said, and I could see his head nodding.

"It's odd that you hired him now," I pressed.

"We had an opening and his skills were perfect for the job," he answered smoothly.

"Well, good for him."

He was quiet for a few seconds. "Did the two of you have a nice visit? I understand Luke came in while the two of you were talking."

"Yes, Luke did come in because he works here and that's what he is supposed to do."

"Nate feels terrible about the way things happened that night," he said.

I sighed, shaking my head. I knew exactly where the conversation was going. "I already told Nate it wasn't his fault. I don't blame him for the way things happened. It was just an accident."

"You pushed him away though. You were very angry with him in the weeks following you coming out of that coma."

"I was angry in general," I told him. "I was angry with Nate because of the fight we had before the accident."

"Couples fight," he answered. "It's part of a relationship. He told me you were fighting over what to eat for dinner."

"It was much more than that, Dad."

"Of course. It's always the little things that trigger a fight, but little things can be fixed."

I slowly shook my head. "It was a lot of little things that turned into a big thing. If we had not broken up that night, we would have eventually."

"I think you've had some time and it might be wise to revisit that relationship. You never truly got closure. You two had an argument and never got the chance to talk about it."

"Dad, I appreciate you trying to play counselor, but Nate and I are over. I don't love him. I would like to remain friends, but I don't want that relationship with him anymore. I wasn't happy. I felt stifled. He expected me to be someone I wasn't and I couldn't keep pretending anymore."

I heard the sigh and knew a lecture was coming. I had heard it before and I would hear it again many more times before I lived up to my father's idea of what my life should look like. "Bree, you are a bright, young woman. You've always been carefree and while I encouraged that when you were younger, it's time to start looking towards your future.

What do you see yourself doing in a year? In five years? Do you really think dabbling in painting is a future?"

I tried not to be insulted. He had never truly appreciated my art, which was why I'd always felt like it wasn't great. Luke was impressed by it. His approval mattered more to me than my father's. "I see myself operating an art gallery. It isn't going to be one of those stuffy galleries that require appointments and only allow established artists to be featured. I want to have an eclectic selection that appeals to the masses and not just the elite."

"Is that really feasible? Art is so subjective. Galleries go under all the time. What is popular today will be out of date tomorrow."

"I know. I get it. I need to try. I thought about it a lot and this is something I really want to do. If it fails, I will at least have had the satisfaction of trying."

"I suppose," he said, with resignation. "I do hope you have a backup plan."

I shrugged. "I don't know that I do. Not yet."

"What about Nate? He is a good man. Why not talk to him about this gallery business."

I rolled my eyes behind my dark shades. One of the benefits of the glasses was no one could really see my eyes. I could be dead asleep, and no one would know it.

"Because Nate thinks it is a silly idea. Nate is the one who held me back from doing it before. You two are a lot alike, which is probably why you like him so much. He wants me to focus on having a family and stepping into the role of a dutiful wife that hosts the best parties and is president of the PTO. I'm not that woman."

"But you could be."

"I don't want to be."

I could see him looking at me. "You are young, but not that young. I'm afraid I might have spoiled you a bit too much. I've made it okay for you to frolic about without a care in the world. You are twenty-five. It's time to start thinking about the rest of your life."

Taking a deep breath, I put down my fork. He wasn't being mean. He was trying the tough love thing. "I'm not frolicking, Dad. I've just been brought back to life and I plan on using every minute I have to enjoy the life I've been given. I learned the hard way that these things we take for granted, like sight, are really precious gifts that we could lose at any time. Spending one moment pregnant and pretending to dote over a man I don't love is the last thing I'm going to do. I want to be with someone who loves me for me. I want to be with someone that supports me, even if my ideas are a little wild and unconventional. I want someone who makes me feel alive."

"Nate loves you. Nate would support you. Relationships require both give and take. A good relationship requires some compromise. He would likely support your hobbies if you were willing to take a more serious approach to other matters."

"Art is not my hobby!" I said, my voice raised now. "It is my passion. My calling. So is traveling and sightseeing. I want to get out and do things. I don't want to play house. Not yet. I'm not saying I don't want that in the future, but I definitely don't want it with Nate. We aren't compatible and I wouldn't make him happy. He isn't a bad guy, but he isn't for me."

Heavy silence was my answer, and I was guessing he didn't approve of my outburst, as he would call it.

"And you think Luke is?" He asked in a way that made it sound like he had just smelled something horrible.

"Maybe," I answered honestly. "I think he could be."

He sighed. "I thought you two were putting all that to rest."

"We put it on hold while I got better."

"And now that you are, what happens next?"

I shrugged. "I'm not sure yet."

"He's not going to be working here much longer. There is no need for you to have a caregiver. You can see. He was only here to take care of you and now you don't need taking care of."

"No, I suppose I don't, but I'm not a hundred percent quite yet. I would like him to be around for a little longer."

"What if he doesn't want to be around?" he questioned. "We've already spoken about it. He's actively seeking employment elsewhere. He'll also be moving out of the cottage."

I felt my heart skip a beat. I knew it was coming, but hearing my father say it shook me. I had come to depend on Luke. I loved having him nearby. I was growing more independent by the day, but I liked hanging out with him.

"I guess we'll cross that bridge when we come to it."

"Are you sure you actually have feelings for him? You were in a vulnerable state. Maybe the feelings were born out of that vulnerability and are not the real thing. Now that you are healing, you might feel differently about the man."

"I don't think so. I care about him and I know he cares about me."

"Of course, he does," he said, as if it was completely obvious. "But you are a beautiful woman with connections and a significant amount of wealth."

"He isn't like that, Dad," I argued. "He could have left a long time ago, but he stuck around."

"I hate to remind you, but he almost didn't."

"He was going through something that had nothing to do with me," I defended. "He's still here. He is the one that has helped me the most during this difficult time. He was there for me even when we didn't think I would ever get my sight back. I think that says a lot."

"He was being paid to be there for you," he quipped.

I frowned. "That isn't nice. You don't know Luke. If you took the time to know him, you would see what I see in him. He's a great guy.

He's kind and loving, and gentle. He supports me. He helps me. That's what I want. I want someone that will be my friend and my champion."

My father's long sigh told me he wasn't convinced. "I just hope you'll keep an open mind while you get through this next phase of your recovery. I'm sure that you've seen Luke now and that might be what is pushing you towards him, but remember, looks are fleeting."

I scoffed. "First of all, I'm not judging the man by his appearance. Second of all, I'm not that shallow, thank you. And for that matter, Nate isn't exactly ugly. It isn't about looks, Dad. It's about the man."

Luke was one fine looking man, there was no doubt about that. I had taken a lot of time studying his face and trying to see his expressions. I wasn't able to make out the little nuances all that well, but his smile was beautiful and he had that southern cowboy thing going for him. It was boyish, handsome, and made butterflies take flight in my stomach. The fact that I hadn't gotten to truly appreciate that face as he had been looking at me with that smile this whole time was a real shame.

If I was wowed by that smile with my horrible vision, I could only imagine what other women would see when they looked at him. He said he had done some modeling. During my blind time, I had assumed he was a catalog model. Seeing him now, I had a feeling he was being modest. The man was smoking hot. Mel had told me, and I had not fully understood. I couldn't wait until I could truly see him.

My dad would have to learn to live with my choices. It was my life and I was going to be very selfish about what I wanted and what I knew would make me happy. I wasn't interested in doing what everyone else thought I should do.

Chapter Eight

Luke

I STEPPED OUTSIDE THE cottage with the cup of coffee I had made. I was taking my time, giving Bree some alone time with her painting. I imagined she was already up in her old room, painting away. It was part of the process of her gaining the independence she had been craving. It was her time. I would go over in a bit and check on her. If she needed me sooner, she knew she could call.

The sound of male voices got my attention. That wasn't normal. It was too early for the gardener or the pool company. With my coffee in hand, I started walking towards the main house. Something told me to stick to the shrubs that provided a modicum of cover. I recognized one of the voices. It was Paul. I rounded the curve that separated the cottage from the open patio area off the main house and immediately shrank into the tall arborvitaes.

It was Paul and Nate. It seemed a little early for a visit, especially considering they worked together and would be together at the office. Something felt off. I crept a little closer to better hear what was being said. Yes, I was an eavesdropper and yes, I was invading their privacy.

"She looks good," I heard Nate say. "Really good."

"She has made a miraculous recovery," Paul agreed.

"Has she said any more about me?" Nate asked.

I frowned. I knew there was more to his sudden reappearance in her life. He wanted her back. "We talked about it last night at dinner. She's working through some things, but I think she will come to her senses."

My heart raced. Anger coursed through my veins.

"Good. That's very good. I know she and I had some problems, but I think we can work through them."

"She mentioned she wanted to go out to that steakhouse she loves," Paul said. "Maybe you could ask her to dinner."

I had to bite my tongue to keep from saying anything. Paul was trying to push Nate and Bree back together. I knew he didn't like me, but damn, I didn't think he would sneak around behind both our backs. He wasn't listening to what Bree wanted. It was the same thing he did while she was suffering with the blindness. He ran roughshod over her. I wanted to stand up for her. I wanted to tell Paul to back off.

"I'll do that," Nate said. I could just imagine the smug look on his face. "When? Should I ask her tonight?"

"Maybe give it a few days," Paul answered. "She is still coming to terms with her new life and she is still working through the blurriness. Maybe a week."

"Thank you, Paul. Thank you. I promise, I will treat her right. I know she will love me again. She needed some space and I get that now. I will give her the space she needs. I will try and be more involved with her art."

"That's a good plan. That crazy girl of mine wants to open an art gallery."

They both laughed. I closed my eyes, fighting back the anger. They were making fun of her. Nate didn't respect her. They were working to manipulate her. I was furious. I wanted to walk over there and kick his ass. The fucker was just playing her. He was going to try and win her back pretending to be something he wasn't, and once he trapped her, he would squash her spirit.

"I better get going. I don't want to be late. Turns out my boss is a real stickler for timeliness."

They laughed again. I rolled my eyes at the stupid joke. I walked back to the cottage, angry as hell and not sure what to do about it. I dumped out the rest of my coffee. My stomach was churning. I waited another fifteen minutes, trying to calm my anger and make sure Paul was gone. I didn't think I could look the man in the eye and not want to tell him I thought he was a jerk. He was totally fucking with his daughter, disrespecting her independence and her dreams. I understood where he was coming from, but he needed to back off and listen to her.

I tentatively opened the glass doors, hoping like hell that Paul wasn't there. I told myself that he was my employer and I couldn't unleash my fury on him. I had to bite my tongue. I had to remember he was her father and I didn't get a say in her life. Not yet.

As I walked through the empty kitchen, I ran into the housekeeper coming out of the living room. "Is Bree upstairs?" I asked.

The woman smiled. "Yes, she is. She's been singing all morning."

That made me smile. "Good."

"She reminds me of her mama."

That surprised me. "You knew her mother?"

The woman's face softened. "I did. I have worked for the family for almost thirty years. Since before they even lived in this big house."

That softened my opinion of Paul just a little. I liked that he had some loyalty. It said something about a man when he had an employee that stuck around for that long. He obviously treated her well. "I'm going to head up."

She nodded and went on her way. I heard the singing as soon as I crested the top of the stairs. She was singing along to what I thought could be a Taylor Swift song. When she hit a high note, I had to slap my hand over my mouth. I stood in the hall, listening to the sound of her singing for several minutes, until the song was over.

"Good morning," I said.

She spun around, her dark shades on and a paintbrush in her hand. There was a splotch of blue paint on her cheek. "Hey!"

"I see you're hard at work."

"I am. I can see you."

I laughed. "More or less than yesterday?"

"I can see you are wearing what I think are jeans and I'm going to guess a black t-shirt."

I nodded. "I am. What else do you see?"

"I can see you smiling," she said.

"I am smiling," I said, walking closer. "I am over the moon to see you looking so happy."

"Come closer. I want to see if I can see your eyes yet."

I stepped close and she was staring at my face. There were mere inches between us. When she made a move to lift the glasses, I started to tell her not to, but quieted my protest. Her stunning blue eyes were focused on mine. For the first time, I could see her seeing me. I don't think either of us breathed. I couldn't even move.

"Can you see them?" I whispered.

"I can. They are a stunning shade of blue."

I released the breath I was holding. "Put your glasses back on."

She smiled and pulled them back over her eyes. "Yes, sir."

"How is the vision?"

"It's a little blurry, but I can see colors without the damn glasses on. I'm so anxious to see color."

"Soon, very soon. How about the headaches?"

She scrunched up her nose. "It only bothers me after I've been painting for too long."

"Make sure you're taking those rests like Ellis told you," I lectured.

"I know, I know."

"Alright. So, I already know you didn't eat. Why don't you take a break and let's have some breakfast?"

She laughed. "You take such good care of me."

"I try."

The rest of the day was spent lounging, with me doing my best to keep her engaged with me instead of trying to use her eyes to paint all the time. I knew she loved to paint, and I wanted her to do it, but she need to give her eyes a break.

My attempt to distract her had run its course. We were back in the room and she was back at the easel. I settled into the chair and watched her paint. I let myself imagine a future with her. Her painting and me watching as we lounged around on a Sunday morning.

"Knock, knock," the voice from the man I loathed floated into the room.

I flinched, lifting my head to look at him. He was holding a bouquet of white daisies. I wanted to knock the dude on his smug ass. I looked over at Bree. She had a bright smile on her face. How could she not see what he was doing!

"Nate!" she exclaimed. "Did you bring me flowers?"

I got to my feet. I wasn't not going to sit by and watch him manipulate her. "What the hell are you doing?" I snapped.

Nate's attention was on me. "Sit down. You're the nurse. You don't get a say in this."

"Excuse me?" I snarled walking towards him. "You're the ex. You don't get to do this to her."

"Do what, bring her flowers? You need to get over yourself."

We stood, chest to chest. I was praying he would push me. I wanted to hit him so bad. I would love to see him taken down a few pegs.

"She doesn't want you, so leave."

"Excuse me," Bree interrupted, as she grabbed my shoulder and yanked me back.

"Your boy toy needs to figure out where he belongs," Nate said, with a smirk on his face.

I lunged, ready to knock him on his ass. Bree interfered, standing between the two of us.

"Stop it," she ordered.

"I think you need to check yourself, nurse man," Nate said.

"Fuck you."

"Luke, go wait downstairs, please," Bree asked.

"Yeah, Luke. Go to your corner," Nate said, with a grin.

"Nate, shut up," Bree growled.

Not wanting to risk Bree getting hurt in a scuffle, I walked out of the room, heading downstairs. I hated that she had chosen him over me. I'd just seen a serious glimpse of my future. Nate was her boyfriend. I was the nurse. I walked into the sitting room, but I couldn't sit. I paced the room, wanting to know what was going on upstairs.

I realized I had probably just fucked myself. Not only would I be fired as her nurse, she would be kicking me out of her life. At least as her nurse I had a chance to be with her, and as I saw it, protect her from Nate. If she fired me, I couldn't do that.

After I waited for what felt like forever, I'd had enough. What the hell was I doing? I wasn't a dog. I didn't get ordered to sit and stay. I had more pride than that. I walked out of the house and headed for the cottage. I should have seen it coming. I should have known I didn't have a chance in hell to be with a woman like Bree. She was way out of my league.

I was the asshole. I was the one who had taken advantage of her. She needed me and what happened between us was very real for me, but she only needed a warm body. Nate wasn't there for her and I slid right in. I had been the consolation prize while Nate waited to see how things worked out. Now that Bree was on her way to being healthy and happy, Nate was ready to swoop back in.

I should have left when we learned the surgery was a success. She didn't need me. As much I wanted to get away from my mother, I felt like I had run right into another unhealthy situation. I tried to tell myself it wasn't that. I had been wrong. I had fallen into old habits and now I was going to pay the price.

Chapter Nine

Bree

I WASN'T SURPRISED to find that Luke was gone. I was still trying to figure out where that little episode had come from. Luke was always so soft spoken, and his outburst had both shocked and angered me. I didn't like feeling as if I was property to be fought over. I didn't do the jealous thing. While it was flattering, it wasn't going to work for me.

I didn't know what I was going to say to him and decided to let him stew for a while. I needed to take some time and figure out what it all meant. Nate was only trying to be nice. I thought the flowers were a sweet gesture. They were definitely unworthy of Luke's violent reaction.

"Bree?"

I turned to see one of the new housekeepers coming my way. "Yes?"

"Your father called and wanted me to let you know he won't be home until late. Do you want me to make you some dinner?"

I smiled. "No thank you, I can fend for myself."

She nodded and disappeared into the kitchen. I wondered if Nate had called my dad the minute he left to tell him what had happened. My dad was probably already plotting to throw Luke out on his ass.

I needed to handle the situation myself. My father already thought I was a fragile flower that couldn't make decisions for herself. I couldn't leave a mess for him to cleanup. I walked out of the house, not even sure if Luke was going to be at the cottage. He might have already packed his things and left.

The cottage was dark when he opened the door. Dark didn't work for me. "Can you turn on some lights?" I asked.

"What are you doing here, Bree?"

"We need to talk," I said.

He opened the door wider and turned on several lights. I stepped inside and closed the door behind me. He was standing in front of me. As usual, my vision was especially blurry. It always was at the end of the day.

"Did your boyfriend leave?" he asked.

"Don't do that. Don't act like a jealous boyfriend."

"I'm not."

"You are."

"Bree, you know I care about you. I want us to have a chance but if you go back to him, where does that leave us?"

"You are the one who ended things."

"So you could figure out what you wanted!" he practically shouted. "I love you. I've told you that before. Nothing has changed for me."

I shook my head. "Pretty convenient timing, don't you think?"

"What's convenient?" he snapped.

"You declaring your love for me. You are acting like a jealous kid. You want the toy that you dropped now that someone else is showing interest."

I could see his mouth drop open. "That is bullshit! I told you before how I felt. I'm not the one trying to manipulate you."

"Aren't you? We've been home for days and you have yet to make a move. You haven't mentioned our future. Nothing. Now all of a sudden, you decide you love me."

"It's never changed," he said.

"I can't do this," I told him.

"Bree, I don't like him. I'm not going to hide that. We have all instincts and this guy triggers mine."

"Why?" I asked. "Is it because of what I told you about him?"

"No," he answered, but the way he said it told me there was more to it.

I took a step back, physically and metaphorically. I could hear the sincerity in his voice. I might not know what he looked like, but I felt like I knew him. He wasn't the kind of man who manipulated people. He was honest and kind. I believed him when he said he cared about me.

I tried to look at this from his point of view. He was going to be out of a job. He was on the verge of losing his home, and he thought he was going to lose me. Suddenly, I felt his fear and uncertainty. He needed to feel safe.

"I'm sorry," I said.

"For?"

"I think I should have tried to understand the situation a little better before I reacted."

"I don't know what that means," he said, exhaustion in his voice.

"It means, our relationship is changing. When I couldn't see you, I listened to your voice and could feel your mood through your breathing. With my sight back, I overlooked the obvious. You're feeling a little lost, am I right?"

"I don't know. I'm telling you the absolute truth when I say I love you, Bree. I know we've only known each other for a short while, but it's the way I feel. I'm happy for you, I truly am, but I'm not sure where I fit into your life now. You had a life before I came along, and that life is still waiting for your return."

"I do have a life, but I don't want to go back to my old life. I have a new life in front of me. I'm going into that life with a new outlook. I don't want any of that baggage from my old life."

"I see," he said in a tight voice.

I smiled and walked towards him. I reached out, my hand resting on his bicep. "I don't think you do."

Before he could say anything, I kissed him. He protested for about half a second before his arms wrapped around me and pulled me in close. The damn glasses got in the way. I reached to take them off. "Don't," Luke said. "Wait."

He stepped away from me and turned off the lights. "Leave one, I said."

He flipped on the small lamp on the end table. I smiled and pulled off the glasses, putting them on the same table with the lamp. I turned to look at him, pissed that I couldn't see him. I wanted to look into his eyes. I wanted to see all the little details of his face.

"Better?" he asked.

"I wish I could see you."

"You can see me."

"Not like I want to," I pouted.

His hands rested on my cheeks. "Soon. Soon you can see every last inch of me."

I smiled at the thought. "You know I'm an artist," I said.

He nodded before dropping a kiss on my nose. "I do know that."

"Artists really love the human body—nude."

He laughed. "Is that a requirement for being an artist?"

"Maybe."

"Look, Bree, I appreciate you trying to make me feel better—"

I didn't let him finish the sentence. I pounced. I kissed him, pushing him backwards with the force of it. His arms were around me. I pushed him backwards until he hit the couch and stumbled. He fell backwards. He kept his arms around me and pulled me on top of him as his back landed on the couch. I didn't stop my attack.

The need I felt was overwhelming. I loved that I could see him, even if it was only in shadows. I ran my hands over his hair and reached down for the hem of his shirt. I yanked it up before pressing my mouth to his warm skin. His hands were sliding down my sides until he yanked my shirt up. I sat up, straddling him and lifting the shirt over my head. I reached behind me and unhooked my bra. I needed skin on skin. It had been too long.

Leaning down, my hair brushing over his shoulder, I kissed him as if my life depended on it. I ground my lower body against his. I could feel the erection straining against his jeans and I slid down his thighs, making room for my hands to undo his pants. His fingers undid the button on my shorts. I hopped off him and stripped off my shorts and panties. I could see movement on the couch and hoped like hell he was taking off those jeans. I looked down at him and saw a blur of skin. He was naked and I couldn't see him.

It was frustrating as hell, but I would worry about that later. Just then, there were more pressing matters that required my attention. I straddled him once again. I was ready for him and didn't want to wait another second to have him deep inside me.

Adjusted myself over him and with one move, I slid onto his shaft. His hands rested on my hips, letting me take complete control. I began to move, straining to see his face, but having to settle for his blurry image.

Riding him slow and deep, I relished in the feel of him inside me. I closed my eyes and leaned my head back. There was something to be said for relying on my tactile senses and forgetting all about trying to see.

"Don't stop," he whispered.

Moaning, I rolled my head to the side. "I'm not going to."

There was no rush. We were all alone and I wanted to take full advantage of it. Part of me needed to prove to him he was the man I wanted. I probably should have used words, but I craved his body. I moved faster, chasing the orgasm I desperately needed. I bent low to kiss him before the need to move had me sitting up once again.

His grip on my hips intensified. He began to push and pull me over him as if I wasn't moving fast enough. Soon, we were in a race. I feared I would fall off the man bucking beneath me. I reached out and held onto the couch and rode him hard and fast.

"Ohh," I cried, feeling the breaking point coming.

"That's it," he grunted. "That's it."

I felt the explosion burst over me, flooding my body with ecstasy. I gasped, sucking in air as he burst inside me. I cried out, moaning and whimpering as pleasure wrapped me up in a vise so tight it felt like I would pass out.

Then I couldn't take it any longer. The moment the orgasm released me, I collapsed onto his chest. His arms wrapped around me, holding me close. I always felt so safe in his arms. He made me feel protected and cherished.

"Wow," he breathed.

I laughed with my mouth against his neck. "Wow, indeed."

"Bree as much as I like doing that with you, I don't want to get ahead of ourselves."

"What do you mean?"

"I mean, what I feel for you is real. I want you. Fuck, do I want you, but I don't want to rush into anything. You're starting this new journey and I don't want to push you in any particular way."

Leaning my face up, I kissed his jaw. "I get it and I don't want to rush into anything either, but can we do this on occasion while we figure things out?"

His deep chuckle vibrated through me. "I would love to, but I don't want things to get mixed up. I don't want you to ever feel like I am using you for that."

"I know," I assured him. "I know things are weird right now, but this is real for me too. Nate is a friend. Please have enough faith in me to know I'm not that naïve. I can think for myself. I can be friends with someone without jumping into bed with them."

His fingertips trailed up and down my spine. "I'll try to do better, but I'm not ever going to change my opinion of him. I trust my gut and maybe it is just me, but I don't like the guy."

I smiled, sensing there was still some underlying jealousy there. "Okay.

Chapter Ten

Luke

I DIDN'T WANT TO MOVE. Her breasts were pressed against my chest, making me want her all over again. I couldn't get enough of the woman. I hated that I had fallen so hard for a woman I shouldn't be able to have. She shouldn't love me. She was meant for so much more in this life than I could possibly give her. She was a woman that could have the whole world. I was a nothing guy from Texas, homeless and jobless.

"Bree, I know you have a lot going on and I don't want to pressure you, but will you give me a heads up if you want this to end. I will respect your decision, but please, please warn me."

"You are sounding very insecure, mister. Have you seen you?"

I laughed. "Have you seen me?"

"I've seen enough of you."

"I am more than my looks," I told her.

She gave me a kiss before pushing off my body. I couldn't help but look at the beautiful breasts in front of me. Her cheeks were flushed, and her hair tousled. "You are so much more than your looks. That's the beauty of it, don't you see? I got to know you without knowing what you looked like. I fell for the man you are, not your looks. They are a bonus."

I smiled, appreciating the words. "I like that."

"So, do I, but I need to get back to the house. My dad will probably be home soon and the last thing I want him to see is me sneaking back in. I don't think he'll be pleased knowing where I've been."

I scoffed. She had no idea just how angry he would be. It would ruin his plans to get her back with Nate. "I'll walk you back."

"We should probably get dressed first," she teased.

I laughed. "I think I like you better in your birthday suit."

"I'm sure I will like you better in your birthday suit."

She climbed off me and when she started to feel around for her clothes, I realized her sight in the dark was still very dim. I handed her the clothes without saying a word. We each dressed before I handed her the glasses. I turned on the lights and took a look at her, making sure everything was in the right place.

"Good?" she asked.

"Perfect."

I walked her back to the house but stopped at the door. She could see well enough and didn't need me to walk her to her bedroom. "I'll see you tomorrow?"

"Yes."

"And if I have a visitor?"

"I'll leave," I growled. I can't stop you from being friends with him, but I sure as hell don't have to be."

She smiled, reaching up to touch my face. "Thank you. I appreciate that."

Giving her a quick kiss, I headed back to the cottage. I made myself a can of soup and sat down on the couch I had just been ridden on. That made me smile. I couldn't help but feel a tiny bit glib. Nate thought he was making the moves on her, but I was the one that had her riding me.

I went to bed early with the scent of her still clinging to my skin. I was going to fight for her. I would be good to her. I would be the man she needed and deserved. I couldn't offer her a mega-mansion, but I could offer her unconditional love. There was a still chance she could lose her sight again. I didn't think Nate would stick by her if that happened.

I fell asleep with her taste on my lips and her scent on my skin. I could almost feel her beside me. I dreamed about the two of us together on a beach somewhere far away.

It was the shrill ringing of my phone that pulled me from the blissful dreams way earlier than I wanted to be awake. I groaned, reaching out to stop the offending noise. I pushed the button on the side, immediately quieting the obnoxious noise. I tossed the phone back on the nightstand and tried to go back to sleep. The damn phone started ringing again.

I rolled to my side and grabbed the phone again. It was barely after six. I recognized the number as one from Dallas. "Are you fucking kidding me?" I growled. My mother needed to get a grip.

"Mom," I answered the phone. "What the hell? You know I'm not in your time zone."

"Is this Luke Turner?" I heard a male voice ask.

"This is Luke Turner. Who's this?" I could feel bad news coming. I knew the tone. I knew the formality of making a call about a person's loved one.

"This Dr. Brunner," he said. "I'm currently treating your mother. You are listed as her next of kin."

I nodded, then remembered he couldn't see me. "Yes. What's going on?"

"Your mother is suffering from kidney failure. I've started her on dialysis, but I'm afraid there has been significant damage."

"Kidney failure?" I repeated. "How? I don't understand."

"I don't know the exact cause, but I believe it is likely a side effect of the medications she has been on for the last ten years. I don't want to point fingers, but if she had been seeing a primary care doctor, this could have been avoided. There is testing that should have been done."

"I see," I said, retracing the meds I had given her over the years. The prescriptions were in her name and none of it seemed suspect.

He cleared his throat. "Your mother has some other problems as well. We are currently monitoring her levels closely. This is a very serious situation."

"I understand," I said, feeling a little numb.

"Will you be coming to see her?"

I sighed. "I'm not sure," I said honestly. "I need to take care of some things here."

"Is there another family member that can be here?" he asked.

"I'm sorry, no. I'm it. I'll check in later this afternoon and see how she responds to the dialysis."

"I'll let the nurse know to expect your call," he said.

"Thank you for calling."

I ended the call and put the phone back on the nightstand. "Holy shit," I breathed.

I couldn't believe she was truly sick. It confirmed what I had suspected for some time. There was no way a doctor would prescribe her something that would kill her kidneys. There would have been tests. She was likely getting meds from someone off the street. My mother was smart. She would know what to do to kill her kidneys. For her sake, I hoped the damage wasn't permanent. She wanted to be sick, but I didn't believe she wanted to die.

The doctor had sounded shocked and then irritated with my response to his dire news. No one would understand the situation. It was something no one without intimate knowledge of our family would understand. I certainly didn't want to explain it.

I should go. She was truly sick. There was a very real possibility she could die. A good son would go to her. A good son would be on the next plane to Texas. Despite all the drama that happened between me and my mom, I did love her. It was an odd dynamic. I didn't necessarily like the woman all that much with the current status of our relationship, but I didn't want her dead.

She was my mom. "Fuck, fuck, fuck."

I flopped back onto the bed and stared up at the ceiling. If I went back to Texas, I knew I would be there for days, maybe even longer. Things with Bree were at a turning point. Her sight was getting better by the day. I wanted to be around when her sight fully returned.

If I was being honest, I didn't want to leave a clear path for Nate. The snake was lurking. Once I was gone, there would be no one standing in his way. Paul would encourage them to go out. Nate would turn on the charm, treat her to that steakhouse dinner they were talking about and try to rekindle the old flame.

Though I knew what Bree said, and I believed she did want to be with me, Nate offered comfort and familiarity. He offered her the approval of her father. Bree and Paul had a close relationship. I didn't want to get in the middle of that. I wasn't sure how I would handle the Paul situation, but I was hoping once Bree declared she wanted to be with me, Paul would fall in line.

I grabbed my phone and pulled up my mom's number. I was probably going to regret it, but I called her.

"Hello," she answered, her voice weak.

"Mom, it's Luke."

"Oh son," she moaned. "Is that you?"

That was the extra drama. "Yes, Mom. I just spoke with your doctor. What happened?"

"I told you I was sick," she complained. "You didn't believe me."

"You are sick, but how did it get this far?" I wasn't expecting an answer. Whatever she told me would be a lie.

She coughed. "It's the medicine," she whispered. "That other doctor was trying to kill me. I think I'll sue."

I rolled my eyes. It would only take a few blood tests and a quick check of her medical records to figure out something was off. Her little secret would be out of the bag. She would likely be the one prosecuted for doctor shopping. I wasn't sure if I would be implicated in the mess. "You need to do what the doctors tell you. Don't mess around with this."

"I'm doing what I can," she moaned. "Will you be here later today?"

"No," I said, closing my eyes.

"Oh dear, that girl won't let you leave today? Tell her it is a family emergency. Tomorrow is fine."

I shook my head. "I won't be there tomorrow either."

"What do you mean?" she asked, that familiar anger and bitterness was in her voice.

"I mean I have obligations here," I answered. "I can't just pick up and leave every time you call."

"Well, I didn't call this time. My doctor did. The doctor that is treating my life-threatening illness, but don't let me get in the way of your little girlfriend. I guess this is you living your life. I didn't realize it meant you were going to truly abandon me. Apparently, I will die alone."

"Mom, I have to handle things here. You're in good hands there. I will call later and see how you are doing. There is nothing to say you can't rebound from this with a little rest."

"You know I can't sleep when I'm in the hospital. I need to be home where I feel comfortable. If you were here, you could take care of me. But I know, I know, you're living your life."

It was the beginning of one of her well-executed guilt trips. She was getting better at them. "I'll call later. Goodbye Mom."

I hung up before she could say anything else. There was no point in staying on the phone. Bree had her appointment in two days. Once I knew for sure how Bree's recovery was going, I would decide whether or not to go home for a visit. I wasn't going to let her rope me in to being her nurse. I would check on her and put her in a facility if it turned out she was going to need long-term care.

That would go over about as well as a lead balloon. I got up and hopped in the shower. I was up. I wasn't going back to sleep. I hoped Bree was up for something fun. I needed a distraction.

Chapter Eleven

Bree

I WAS ANXIOUS. CRAZY anxious. I had barely slept a wink last night in anticipation of the appointment with Ellis. It was just shy of two weeks since I'd had the surgery. My vision was still very blurry. I was terrified that this was as good as it was going to get. I told myself I had to be happy with what I got, but it was still disappointing.

But I had made such crazy plans. I had planned on painting and opening an art gallery and traveling the world. Technically, I was still legally blind. I would never drive again. I would never see true colors again. I would never see the little nuances of Luke's face.

Staring out my bedroom window, my dark shades in place, I knew I should be looking at the bright side of things. I wouldn't have to wear the sunglasses much longer. At least then I could see the shadows in the bright light of day.

"Hey there," I heard my father say.

I slowly turned. He was excited for the appointment. "Hi," I said offering him a smile.

"I've got some bad news," he said.

"What? What's happened?"

He chuckled. That was not the reaction I expected. "I'm sorry. I was being dramatic. I've got an emergency meeting with my board. I won't be able to make your appointment. I'm afraid I need Nate with me as well."

I tried to hide my relief at the knowledge Nate would not be going along for the appointment. He had sprung that little tidbit of information on me the night before. He claimed Nate wanted to go along to support me. I didn't want Nate there. I didn't need or want his support. I didn't tell Luke about Nate going because I didn't want the fight. Now, I wouldn't have to. That was one giant bullet dodged.

"Well, that's a bummer," I said, with an extra dose of sadness. Truthfully, I wasn't upset at all that he couldn't make it. He always made me feel like I was broken, like we were at a fixer's office. Ellis had done her job. My eyes had failed me.

"I'll try and catch up with you after the appointment."

"I'm sure you won't be missing anything. It's just a checkup."

He stepped closer, putting his hands on my shoulders. "I'm proud of you, Bree. You've been so strong, and I am so proud of you."

I smiled. "Thanks, Dad."

"I've got to run."

"Bye Dad," I said, with a wave.

I listened for the front door. Once I heard it close, I headed for the kitchen. I was a little surprised Luke wasn't at the house yet. I made my coffee and took it outside to sit on the patio. I listened to the birds singing and chatting back and forth. I could smell the chlorine from the pool and longed to jump in. I was going to ask if I could go swimming yet. I was dying to get in the water.

Finally, I saw a shadowy figure coming my way and assumed it was Luke.

"Hey gorgeous," I heard him say.

I laughed. "You always say the sweetest things."

He dropped a kiss on top of my head. He rarely touched me unless he knew we were alone.

"I saw him leave," he said, answering my unspoken question. "Is he meeting us at the clinic?"

"No," I told him. "He got called into a meeting."

"Oh," he answered, sounding a little surprised.

He sat down at the table with me and seemed a little subdued.

"Is everything okay?" I asked.

"Yes, fine. I'm anxious for the appointment. I know it's going to go great, though."

"I hope so. I hope she can tell me why I can't see that well. If this is as good as it's going to get, I hope she will just be up front with me. I don't want to keep hoping. If this is it, I will make myself be okay with it."

"Don't lose hope just yet," he said. "She said it could take a couple of weeks."

"It's been almost two weeks."

"And you have had moments of clarity. The key is to rest those eyes. Your poor peepers need a break."

I laughed. "My peepers had three months to rest. Now it's time for them to get busy."

"Did you eat?" he asked, sliding right into caregiver mode.

"I ate some toast. Are you sure there's nothing wrong? You've not sounded like yourself the last couple days."

"It's nothing. My mom is sick, but like I told you before, she's always sick."

"Are you sure it's nothing?"

"I'm here. This is where I want to be."

It wasn't a real answer, but it was all I was going to get. We enjoyed the peace and quiet of the morning before it was time to go. I was anxious and dreading it at the same time. Luke held my hand as we walked into the clinic Ellis was using to see the few patients she had in California. I felt privileged to be one of the few lucky ones that got to call her my doctor. Mel had done some research and discovered she was one of those hotshots that people from all around the world clamored to get into. She had basically fallen into my lap and I had to believe it was fate. I had to believe she had come into my life for a reason.

"This is it," he said, giving my hand a squeeze. We sat down, waiting our turn to be seen. I felt a little ridiculous with the giant glasses on, but figured I wasn't the only one sporting the stylish eyewear.

"Gabrielle Sullivan?" I heard my named called.

Luke stood, never letting go of my hand. We were taken into an exam room with the lights on dim. I took off my glasses, happy to lose the damn things even if it was only for a short time.

"Hi guys," Ellis said, walking into the rather cramped room. I was glad my father skipped the visit. It would have been a little claustrophobic with all of us piling into the room.

"Hi," I greeted her. I felt like I owed the woman so much. Now that I could see her a little better, I realized she was pretty. At least, she had a nice figure. I couldn't make out all the details of her face, but she had black hair and pale skin.

"How are you feeling?" she asked.

"Good. So much better."

"How is the vision?"

I shrugged. "Blurry. Really blurry."

"Are you wearing the glasses?"

"Always," I answered. "I only take them off at night or when the room is darkened."

"Can you see how many fingers I'm holding up?"

I squinted. "Two?"

"Good job. Now?"

I leaned forward. "Seven."

"Yes. Your vision is getting there. I'll do a quick exam, look for any signs of clouding that could be causing the blurriness. I'm sure everything is fine. Have you had any eye pain?"

"Not really. I get headaches in the evening sometimes, but nothing major."

"She paints all day," Luke chimed in.

I turned to scowl at him. "Tattletale."

Ellis laughed. "As long as you are wearing the glasses and not straining your eyes, it's okay."

I sat perfectly still while she shone a light into my eyes and went about checking my vision. She stepped away from me and the black hair with the pale face was gone. "Well?" I asked hopefully.

"I don't see any problems. You can start leaving the glasses off when you are indoors. You'll want to avoid any bright areas, like your solarium, but you can use lights. If your eyes hurt, put the glasses back on. Listen to your body."

"Will I ever see clearly again?"

"I don't see any medical reason why you shouldn't. Give it some time. Some patients see clearly faster than others. This isn't a race. This is you making your way back, one day at a time. I'm not worried."

"What about swimming? Can I go swimming?"

She sucked in a breath. "Not yet. I advise my patients to wait a full six weeks. The risk of an infection is just not worth it."

I let out a long sigh. "Okay. Can I wear normal sunglasses when I am outside?"

Her pretty laugh filled the room. "Yes, but they have to provide true UV protection. This should be a rule all the time. I hate seeing people wear sunglasses that look great but offer no protection. They are not a fashion statement; they are as important as wearing sunscreen."

I nodded. "Absolutely."

"Is there a particular brand?" Luke asked.

"Not necessarily, but I always recommend mirrored glasses. It isn't a necessity, but I'm sure you can find something that is fashionable and effective."

I nodded. "Okay. We'll go shopping right after we leave here."

She laughed. "Great. I will refer you to one of my colleagues for another follow-up in four weeks. If there are any issues or concerns before then, just give me a call."

I hopped off the exam table and while I knew it was customary to shake her hand, I wanted to hug her. I had been very jealous of her initially, but now that I owed her so much, I couldn't be jealous. Besides, I was confident Luke was into me.

"Thank you again," Luke said, as we walked out of the office.

My ugly glasses were back on as we left the clinic. "Can you please take me to get some new sunglasses at once?"

He chuckled. "Absolutely."

I told him where to go. It had been forever since I had done any shopping. I was dying to go on a serious shopping spree, but for now, I would limit it to some new shades. We spent an hour working with a sales associate to find a couple different pairs. Luke stayed out of the way and acted as my purse holder while I tried on different pairs.

"Thank you," I told him as we walked out of the new store. "I feel a million times better."

"How about your eyes? Is the sun too bright?"

I shook my head. "Not at all. It's time they started to adjust to the light."

My phone rang just as I was getting into Luke's car. I recognized the ringtone. "Hey Dad," I answered, before giving him a quick update on the situation.

"Do you feel like grabbing some lunch at Nobu?" he asked.

I scrunched up my nose. I couldn't imagine Luke, my Texas boy, enjoying sushi. "I'm beat. I think I'm going to go home and lay down for a bit. Raincheck?"

"Of course, sweetheart. Get some rest and I'm happy to hear the good news."

I slid my phone into my purse and leaned back on the drive home. I was exhausted. All my worrying had turned out to be for nothing. Ellis was certain I would get my vision back. I just had to wait. I wasn't sure I had the patience.

"It's going to be alright," Luke said, reaching across the console to grab my hand.

"I think I was hoping for instant results," I told him.

"I understand it has to be very difficult, but you are doing really well."

"Two weeks," I murmured. "I'm going to give myself two more weeks before I really start freaking out."

He chuckled. "No freaking out. At least you can leave the glasses off in the house. That's a huge step in the right direction."

"It is and I am happy for it. I'm so damn anxious to get back to seeing."

My father agreed to keep Luke on until my vision was completely restored. I hoped Luke saw it as a reprieve and not a longer sentence. I didn't necessarily need a caregiver, but I did like the companionship.

Chapter Twelve

Luke

THE SUN WAS STILL A little too much for Bree's eyes to handle, which meant instead of sitting by the pool on a lazy Saturday afternoon, we were in the solarium. She was anxious to go swimming. I promised I would dive in with her as soon as the doctor gave her the all clear. For now, we were doing more sitting and more waiting.

"I wish I could just make them better," she said.

I turned my head to look at her. She looked so normal, so much like a high-fashion or swimsuit model with her shades on. Her all over tan gave her a healthy glow. "Soon," I told her. "It's getting better little by little."

"How are you?" she asked, looking at me from behind the sunglasses that cost more than I made in a week.

"I'm fine, why?"

"Because I know you and I know something is on your mind."

I smiled. "I'm fine. I'm good."

"Are you worried about the future?"

I shrugged. "Aren't we all a little worried about the future?"

"Yes and no. You can tell me whatever it is."

"I appreciate that. I'm doing just fine."

We sat for a few more minutes. I was spending a little time with her before Mel showed up to take her shopping. It was something I was sure only Mel could do. I didn't really know Bree's style. We'd been very casual the entire time I knew her. Plus, it would do her good to get out and do normal things with her friend.

"Hey guys," Mel's voice filled the quiet solarium. "Well, don't you two look cozy?"

I turned to look up at her. "We are cozy."

Mel took a seat, a huge smile on her face. "I'm so damn excited. I feel like a kid with a ticket to Disneyland in my hand. I cannot wait to go shopping."

"Just remember she needs to keep her glasses on outside," I lectured. "She should be okay in the stores, but if you see her frowning, it means her eyes are straining."

"She is sitting right here," Bree said.

"But you are stubborn, and you don't listen to your body," I told her.

Mel burst into laughter. "You two sound like an old married couple."

I grinned. "We do spend a lot of time together."

"And he takes really good care of me," Bree added.

"Cute," Mel said before jumping to her feet. "Now, let's go. My credit card is burning a hole through my purse."

Bree turned to me with a smile on her face. "Maybe I'll come by later and give you a little fashion show."

"I would like that."

"Will you be around?" she asked.

I slowly nodded. "I have no plans to go anywhere."

She looked at me for several seconds. "Okay, then. I'll see you later."

I walked them to the door, said goodbye and then headed back to my cottage. She was very intuitive, and I knew she was sensing my stress and worry. I was trying to play it cool, but it was clinging to me. I had been up most of the night talking to one of my old friends back in Dallas. He was working in the necrology unit and had checked in on my mother. She was seriously ill.

It had been a week and she didn't seem to be getting any better. Blaine told me he wasn't sure if she would make it. I trusted him. He had graduated from nursing school with me and had been working at the same hospital with me for years. He wasn't an idiot. He knew his stuff. After working with people for years, nurses developed a good sense about who was going to make it and who wasn't. If he thought my mom was truly ill, it had to be very serious.

I was torn. I felt like I was being pulled in two different directions. There was the woman I was in love with who needed me still and then there was my mother who also needed me. I wanted to be there for both of them. I had been trying to tell myself there was nothing I could do for my mom. She was in a good hospital and the staff was taking care of her. She had a team of doctors and nurses providing for her every need.

Every need except her emotional needs. She was depressed and crying every time I spoke with her. She couldn't believe I hadn't jumped on a plane and gone to her right away. I explained the situation to her over and over. It always came down to I loved Bree more than her.

It was a different kind of love and it was a different kind of need. I needed to be with Bree. I felt like shit because I wanted Bree. I was terrified to lose her to Nate and was digging in. It wasn't fair to my mom. It made me feel selfish to choose my happiness over her needs. She didn't let me forget it either. She reminded me at every turn.

I could ignore some of her drama, but the last few days, it was hard to ignore. The guilt was overwhelming. I needed to figure out what I was going to do, or it was going to eat me alive. I sat down on the couch, turned on some lame reality show and found myself dozing off. The lack of sleep all week was catching up with me.

I jerked awake and immediately reached for my phone to check the time. It was just after two. I had slept for two hours. That was unexpected and a testament to my exhaustion. I rubbed a hand over my face and checked for any missed calls or messages. There weren't any, which was a good sign. Everyone at the hospital knew to call me if anything changed with my mother's condition. She was stable, but still in serious condition.

Checking the time, I decided it was time to talk to Lisa. I wasn't sure if she even knew about Mom's condition. I hadn't bothered calling her initially because I assumed it was yet another one of mother's episodes. Lisa didn't want to be bothered with those. This was different. No matter their differences, Lisa needed to know what was going on. I walked outside, sitting in one of the chairs with my back to the sun beating down on the patio area.

"Hello?" Lisa answered. I could hear music in the background and was glad to know I had not woken her.

"Hey, it's me," I said.

"What's up?"

"Mom's sick," I blurted out.

I heard her sigh. "She's always sick, Luke."

"No, Lisa. This is serious. They are still running tests, but her kidneys are failing. She is getting dialysis."

"Oh. Are you still in California?"

"Yes, but I think I should go."

"Luke, why? Is there anything you can do for her? Are you going to give her the dialysis?"

"No, but, she's all alone," I argued.

"She's not alone," she replied. "She's got doctors and nurses and I bet she has managed to get herself a whole team of volunteers that are doting on her. She's in her element. I bet she's happier than she's ever been now that she is finally seriously ill."

"Lisa, this is serious! She could die!"

"I doubt it. I'm sure she's doing something to make them think that. The woman is trying everything she can to get you back there."

"I have to go see her," I breathed the words. I needed Lisa to make the decision for me. I needed someone to tell me what to do.

"No, you don't," she said, and I wanted to shout with glee. "She's only doing this to pull you in. If you go back, she's going to sink her claws in and you will never leave. She'll find another way to get herself back in the hospital and knocking on death's door. That woman will kill herself to control you. Don't do it."

I closed my eyes, shaking my head. "I don't know. This time is different. She's never been this bad before."

"Um, yes, she has. Remember when she took that concoction of vitamins that nearly made her have a heart attack? She is unwell, Luke. Sick. She is sick in the head and she doesn't seem to care about her life. You've done all you can for her. You have to leave her alone. This might be her wake up call."

I wanted to believe it. I wanted to think this near-death experience would be the one that made my mother realize what she was doing was literally going to kill her. "I don't know," I groaned. I felt more confused than I had before I called.

"Is she in the hospital?" Lisa asked.

"Yes."

"Then leave her there. You can do nothing for her."

"She wants to go home," I explained. "She doesn't like being in the hospital."

"Bullshit," Lisa snapped. "She loves being in the hospital. She loves being waited on hand and foot. It's what she lives for."

"She wants to be in her own bed."

"I'm sure she does because then she can eat whatever, whenever she wants. She can sneak those cigarettes we both know she still smokes. She can drink her whiskey and have you there to baby her. She is telling you she wants to go home because she wants you to be her little bitch. She wants you to dote on her and give up your entire life for her. She's manipulating you, Luke. See it for what it is."

"You are being really harsh," I told her.

"I'm being real. I thought she might have changed after all these years. When I went back for my visit, all she could talk about was her. She complained nonstop about you leaving her. She didn't give a shit that we had not seen each other in years. It was you she wanted. I can't explain it, but the woman has fixated on you. Stay away. I'm warning you, Luke, it isn't good for your health to be near that woman. You are lucky she hasn't tried to make you sick."

"She wouldn't want me sick because that would mean I couldn't take care of her," I scoffed.

"Exactly!" she exclaimed.

I blew out a breath. "I don't know. I should probably go home and just see for myself. I'll tell her to snap out of it and then come back to California."

"It's cute that you think you have that kind of nerve," she quipped.

"Are you calling me a pussy?" I snapped.

"I'm calling you a man that has been manipulated by his mother from the very moment he took his first breath. I'm saying she has been fucking with your mind your entire life. It is a miracle you are not seriously damaged. Don't go back. I don't think you are strong enough to get away from her a second time."

I knew she was speaking out of genuine concern for me. "I hear you," I said, feeling completely defeated.

"I love you kid, stay strong."

"I will. Thanks for the pep talk. If she dies though, I'll never forgive myself and I'm warning you now, I'm probably going to blame you a little."

She laughed. "I'm sorry. I don't want you to get hurt. Stay in California. Stay with Bree. Live your life. If mom is truly knocking on death's door, you will know. Then, and only then, do you go see her. If she needs around the clock care, sell the house and put her in a home. Don't do it yourself."

"Bye," I said, and hung up the phone.

I wasn't lying when I told her I would blame her. I would blame her for talking me out of going. Obviously, it would be my own fault, but if my mother died, it was going to be a knife to the heart. I rubbed my temple, shaking my head. I couldn't put it on Lisa. I had to do what I thought was right.

Chapter Thirteen

Bree

I DIDN'T KNOW WHAT to say. Did I tell him I heard the tail end of what sounded like a very dire conversation or did I very quietly backtrack and pretend I never heard a word? I knew there had been something bothering him. From what I gathered, I guessed it was his mother.

He had told me the condensed version of their odd relationship, but listening to his conversation told me it was a lot worse than I thought. I had felt something was off and if I would have had clear sight, I would have been able to see his expression. I would have been able to know for sure if my suspicions were correct. Without being able to see, I had to trust his words.

He had lied. I wasn't sure how that made me feel. "Luke," I said his name.

He jumped up, spinning around and looking at me. "Bree!" he said with surprise. "You're back already."

I smiled. "I am. Contrary to what Mel thought we were going to do, I really wasn't up for a shop until I dropped on my ass. It was that kind of shopping trip."

"Oh. Are you okay?" He stepped forward and I knew he was probably looking for any signs of injury or fatigue. That was Luke. He was always looking out for me.

"I'm fine. I couldn't help but overhear that last bit of your conversation. Are *you* okay?"

"Yes," he answered too quickly. "I'm good. Fine."

"Why are you lying to me?" I asked, growing a little irritated with the games. "I'm not an idiot. I might not be able to see the worry on your face, but I can feel it. And I have been for a few days. What is going on?"

"Bree, it's nothing for you to worry about."

I frowned. I didn't appreciate being dismissed and that is what he was doing. "You expect me to share my life with you. You ask me all the time if I'm okay or what's on my mind. Why can't I do the same for you?"

I heard him sigh. "I just don't want to burden you with my problems."

"You aren't burdening me. If we are going to make a relationship work, it is going to mean we both share. This can't be one-sided."

"Dammit, you are just too good for words."

I laughed. "You say that now, but when we are butting heads, you might feel differently."

"You are just so beautiful," he said.

"Okay, okay, quit trying to change the subject. What's going on? Is it your mom?"

He reached out and took my hand and led me back inside. I waited while he pulled the curtains closed. When the bright light of the day was gone, I took off my sunglasses. I could see his shape a little better than I had two days ago.

"It's my mom," he said.

"What's wrong with her?" I asked.

I could see his head shaking. "She's sick. She's always sick."

"But you said something about her dying. Were you talking to her doctor?"

"I was talking to Lisa. I wanted to let her know about the situation with Mom."

"Is Lisa still in England?"

"Yes."

He was giving me no information. When it came to his mother and his family in general, he was very tight-lipped. "Luke, please tell me what is going on. This seems like a lot more than she's sick."

"She's in the hospital. Her doctor says her kidneys are failing along with some other organ failure."

My mouth dropped open. "Luke, that sounds bad. I'm sorry. That sounds terrible."

"It isn't good."

"Don't you want to be there?" I asked.

He loudly exhaled. "I don't know what to do."

"What do you mean?"

"It's complicated."

"Okay, then we work through it. One step at a time. We will work through it. Why aren't you there?"

"Because you are here," he immediately answered.

"You are not going to see your mother, who is seriously ill, because I'm here?" I clarified.

"Yes and no."

I smiled. The poor man was a mess. I moved to sit next to him on the couch, then reached out and found his hand. I took it between mine like he had done for me so many times. "Yes, because I'm here. But what is the no?"

"It isn't only because of you. This isn't the first time she has been hospitalized."

I nodded. "But this time is different?" I said, sensing there was more to the story.

"This time it's real," he said, sounding like the weight of the world was on his shoulders. "She's getting dialysis. I've talked to a couple of the doctors and with one of the guys I worked with. It's real."

The sadness in his voice was evident. "I'm truly sorry. Is it going to get better?"

"I don't know. I honestly don't know. I guess that's what is bothering me. I don't know what to do."

"If I wasn't here, would you be there?"

"Yes," he answered without hesitation. "But you are here, and this is where I want to be. You are making great progress in your recovery. I need to be here."

"Luke you have helped me more than I can say. You have changed my life in a good way. I would have never gotten this far without you."

"Thank you. That means a lot to me."

"I don't want to be the thing that keeps you from seeing your mother. I can tell you are genuinely concerned. I heard what you said at the end there. I don't want to be the one you blame if something does happen and you aren't there."

"I would never blame you," he insisted.

"You say that, but deep down, you would."

"I'll get through this. I don't want to burden you with it. You have enough on your plate."

"We'll get through this together. I've never been to Texas. I'll go with you. That way you aren't leaving me, and you don't have to feel torn."

"No," he said. "I'm not going to let you do that. You've got to take care of yourself."

"I can take care of myself here or in Dallas. I want to help you, and this is the best option. There is nothing that requires you to stay here and ignore your family obligations. I know you and your mom have a tricky relationship. I don't want to make it any trickier than it already is."

"I can't to do this," he said.

"Luke, you are the one with a lot on your plate. Let me be there for you for once. That's how relationships work. Lean on me. I've been leaning on you for weeks. Let me feel needed. Let me feel like the other half of this relationship instead of just dead weight."

He laughed. "You are not dead weight."

"I have certainly felt like it. You've been everything for me. You've been my eyes, my counselor, my lover and most importantly, my friend. Let me be a little something for you."

His soft laughter warmed my heart. I liked knowing I could make him laugh. "You are more than a little something. I don't know if it's a good idea to have you fly though and I don't want to make the drive."

"I flew home," I reminded him.

"True, but your eyes are still healing."

"If it makes you feel any better, I will text Ellis and ask her if flying is a problem. Trust me, I don't want to risk my eyesight. I'm not going to sacrifice the progress I have made. Let me do this. Please?"

He hesitated. "Your dad might have something to say about it."

"My dad will have a lot to say, but guess what? I'm a big girl. I can go wherever I want, with whomever I want."

"It's not going to be that easy," he insisted.

"No, but it will be fine. When do we leave?"

"I guess this is me getting to see your other side," he said with resignation.

"Yes, it is. What's the weather like? What should I pack?"

He laughed again. "You are a force."

"I am. We're doing this."

"I haven't even decided if I want to go. This could be another one of her stupid, fucking games. Lisa thinks she is trying to mind fuck me. I tend to believe her. Unfortunately, she tends to go to great extremes to get what she wants, and I would not be surprised if she did this on purpose."

"Do you really think she would make herself deathly ill? And what is it she wants?"

"Me," he said, his voice so low I barely heard him. "She wants me there."

I didn't understand it. It confused me. "Like she wants you there because she misses you? It's kind of sweet that she loves you that much."

He groaned. "It isn't love, not the kind of love between mother and son."

I pulled my hand away, suddenly worried about what I had stepped in. "Oh. I, uh, I—" I was speechless. I was a little grossed out. I felt dirty for him.

"No, no, no," he quickly said. "Not like that. Gross."

I let out a sigh of relief. "Thank goodness. I had no idea what to say."

"My mom has this idea that she needs my attention. She is sick, in the head. She knows she has lost that hold over me and this is how she is pulling me back in. If I go there, she is going to lay on a hell of a guilt trip. It's hard to explain how it happens, but I can't fight the pull. If I'm there, she is going to fuck with my head. I don't know if I'm strong enough to walk away. That's why I don't want to go."

I felt so bad for him. I only knew the strong Luke. I only ever saw him as the stalwart man that never flinched when I was freaking out. "I'll drag you away," I told him. "I won't let you get pulled into something that will ultimately hurt you."

"I appreciate the offer, but I just don't know. Lisa thinks it is a really bad idea."

I felt like I needed to choose my words carefully. What I said next could come back to haunt me. I didn't want to do or say anything that would offend him or piss him off. "Luke, I hope I don't regret saying this, but I think I know you pretty well. I think you have been suffering these past few days. It is your nature to care. I wouldn't want you to be any different. You are a very special human. Your sister said you were an empath. You are. It's what makes you, you."

"Thanks," he muttered.

"What I'm trying to say is if you don't go see your mother, you are never going to sleep. You are going to stress yourself out. I believe you are strong enough to walk away from her after you have assured yourself, she is going to be okay."

He was silent for several seconds. "Are you sure you're okay to go with me?"

I grinned. "Absolutely."

"Thank you. Truly. I promise I will take care of you. I hope the trip will only be a day, two at most. We'll be right back here."

I waved a hand. "I've heard there is some good shopping in Dallas. I want to see where you grew up. I want to get to know you better. You know so much about me and I know so little about you."

"Promise me something?" he said.

I shrugged. "That's a loaded statement."

"Don't let her get you down. Don't let her get under your skin. She says things. Ignore them."

I smiled. "I get it. Last time your mother and I talked was different. I was weak. I'm not weak anymore. I can handle myself."

"Okay. Then I guess we better talk to your dad."

I got to my feet. "I can't wait to travel!"

He laughed. "I really wish it was under different circumstances."

"Me too, but we are going to make the best of it."

"I'll meet you over there in about thirty minutes," he said.

"Don't stand me up," I teased.

"I wouldn't think of it."

Chapter Fourteen

Luke

I WATCHED HER WALK away. The woman was too good for me. She was dealing with something huge in her life, yet she was concerned about me. I was overwhelmed. No one had ever cared about me enough to think about my needs. It was strange and sweet, and I wasn't sure how to process it all. To say it gave me the warm and fuzzies was an understatement.

As much as I appreciated her offer, I was hesitant to accept it. I could reject it. I could put my foot down and tell her she wasn't invited. But that would only hurt her. Then again, going to Dallas would almost certainly expose her to some serious drama. My mother was toxic.

Her little impromptu visit had sent Bree into a tailspin. I was terrified my mother would say or do something that would plunge Bree right back into that depression she had barely escaped from. When my mother was in one of her sick modes, she was vicious. She blamed it on the pain of whatever illness she was suffering from.

I could call Ellis and persuade Ellis to tell Bree it was dangerous for her to fly. I could tell Bree I was really bummed, and she would still get to play the supportive friend and I could protect her from my mother. The idea would probably work with any other woman, but I knew Bree. She could dig in. She would insist on getting to Dallas one way or another. It was safer to have her on the flight next to me.

Standing up, I went inside the cottage. I wasn't looking forward to talking with Paul. I knew the man was going to be pissed. He was overprotective of his daughter as it was. Me dragging her to Dallas to deal with my family drama was not going to go over well.

I opened my laptop and did a quick search for flights. It was my obligation to pay for her ticket. It was going to put a serious dent into the savings account I was barely building back up from the last flight home. I cringed at the prices but found two seats out tomorrow morning. If Paul put his foot down and refused to let her go, I was going to be out a few hundred bucks.

Sending the ticket information to my phone, I shut down the laptop. Putting off the talk with Paul wasn't going to make it any better. It was better to get it over and done with. I walked over to the main house and knocked on the glass door. I wasn't going to just walk in—not when I knew there was a good chance Paul was there.

I pulled out my phone and sent a quick text to Bree to let her know I was there if it was a good time. A few seconds later, I saw her coming towards the doors. I put my phone back and waited. "He's in the living room," she said. "I told him I needed to talk to him."

"And? What kind of mood is he in?"

She laughed. "You are way too worried about this. I'm not a little girl."

"You are *his* little girl."

Her warm smile told me she knew that. "But I'm his little girl with a mind of her own and the adult card that says I can go where I want, when I want."

"I hope so," I muttered. "I already bought the tickets."

"What?" she gasped. "You did?" The look on her face was pure joy. I hoped she had that same look when we touched down in Texas and she was exposed to my mother's vitriol.

"I did. Tomorrow morning if you can make it."

"Absolutely," she squealed before clapping her hands together. "My first trip post-accident. I'm so excited. I mean I'm sad that it's under these circumstances, but I'm excited to go and I'm excited to be with you."

That made me feel good, but I wasn't going to get too excited. Bree was her own woman, but Paul could be very stubborn. He could make her feel like she had to stay because he said so. I had witnessed the way he controlled her on numerous occasions.

"Dad?" Bree called out. "Luke's here."

Her father was sitting on the couch, one leg thrown over the other, his glasses resting on the tip of his nose while he read something on his iPad. He had a glass of what I was going to guess was bourbon sitting on the table next to him. He looked up, his eyes going to Bree and then me. He didn't look happy.

"What's this about?" he asked, putting down the tablet. "Is this to tell me you guys are starting up again?"

"No, sir," I answered a little too quickly for Bree's taste apparently. Her sunglasses were off, and she was glaring at me. I bit back the smile. Now wasn't the time to rejoice in that little tidbit of information.

Bree took a seat and gestured for me to do the same. I sat a respectable distance from her on the couch that faced Paul. "Dad, I'm going to Texas with Luke tomorrow," Bree announced.

The look on the man's face would have been funny if it wasn't such a serious situation.

"Pardon me?" he said, his eyes shooting daggers at me before looking at his daughter.

"You heard me," Bree said. "Luke needs to go home, and I would like to go along with him."

"You *need* to go home?" Paul pressed. "To stay?"

"My mother is in the hospital," I explained. "I'm just going back for a day or two to make sure she is doing okay."

Paul shook his head. "There is no reason for you to go," he said, looking at his daughter. "He'll be back. You need to stay and rest, and recover from the surgery."

"It's been two weeks and the only recovery is my eyes. They are taking their sweet time getting back to normal. There is nothing I can do to speed that up. I want to go."

"But flying could be risky," he insisted.

"I flew home a couple days after the surgery. I have sent Ellis an email asking her if it's okay. If she doesn't get back to me, I will call or text her. She said I could call anytime. I'm going to take her up on that."

He shook his head. "It seems very unnecessary. You could stay here and relax. There's nothing for you in Dallas."

"Luke is in Dallas and I want to start traveling more. This is the first step in that direction."

"Why not wait a few more weeks until your sight is back?"

She gave him a look. "Because his mother is in the hospital now. It's really hard to say what might happen in a few weeks. Luke had been a huge source of strength and support for me and I want to be there for him."

I cringed, knowing that was not going to go over well. I wasn't sure what to say or whether I should say anything at all. I wasn't sure what I could add to the conversation without making it worse on either side. "I would appreciate her company," I finally said.

Paul shot me a look that told me he was not happy. "And what is she supposed to do while you are visiting your mother in the hospital? You know how she get in hospitals."

"I'll be okay, dad. I have to get over it eventually. It isn't so bad now that I can see a little."

"I think you need to stay home," Paul said, with a finality in his voice that set my teeth on edge.

Bree wasn't a little girl. He needed to quit trying to control her life. He was acting as if I was taking her away to a third-world country to live the rest of her days. I was the one who had been entrusted with her life the last couple of months. I was the one who dried her tears and made her smile.

"No," Bree said. Her tone was quiet but firm. "I'm going. We leave tomorrow morning."

"Bree!" Paul exclaimed. "You should have talked to me before you made plans."

"Why? I've never asked you to go anywhere before, Dad. Why do you think I have to start doing that now?"

"Because things are different now. What about Nate?"

Bree looked confused. It was my turn to clench my teeth together. Paul was just as manipulative as my mother. "What about Nate?" Bree asked.

"Don't you think you should talk this over with him?" Paul said, as if it was completely reasonable.

"Um, no, I don't," Bree answered. "Nate has nothing to do with this."

I waited for Paul to tell her why Nate had something to do with it. I waited for him to tell her he was working to push the two of them back together. I waited. Paul looked at me and then his daughter.

"I just thought you and Nate were on good terms again, and if you are planning on a trip, the polite thing to do is let him know you will be out of town for a couple days."

"I really don't think it's any of his business, but if it makes you feel better, I'll send him a text," Bree agreed.

"I need to go pack," I said, and jumped to my feet. I didn't want to hear another word about Nate. He was a fucking piece of shit and the fact that Paul didn't see it pissed me off. If he was so worried about his daughter, he should think twice about who he was pushing her towards.

"Me too," Bree said, acting as if she wasn't the least bit bothered by her father's anger.

"That's it?" Paul asked. "You're just going to go?"

"Yes," Bree answered, and walked out of the room behind me.

I headed for the kitchen, anxious to make my escape from Paul. I didn't want to say something I regretted. "You don't have to do this," I said again before I opened the door. "He doesn't want you going. I do understand his concerns."

"I'm not concerned. I want to go. You both need to understand that I'm not going to break. I am going to live my life the way I want. I know you both got comfortable with the quiet, compliant me. That's not who I am, and I didn't like being that person. I don't plan on being that person again."

I couldn't help but smile. I liked the feisty Bree. "Alright. Pack for warm weather."

She smiled again. "I will. What time in the morning?"

"Can you be at the cottage at eight?"

"I'll be there."

I was tempted to give her a quick kiss goodnight, but felt it would only stir the pot if Paul caught us. "I'll see you in the morning. Thank you for doing this. I really do appreciate it."

"I'm excited to go."

I walked back to the cottage and headed in to pack my suitcase. I hadn't asked Bree anymore about Nate, but I wondered if they were talking. Paul had made it sound like they were close. It could have just been his way of trying to get me to back off, but it seemed like there was more to it. I would not be the least bit surprised to discover Nate and Bree had been talking after I went home for the night.

I told myself I didn't have a right to be jealous. She had made it clear she didn't like that possessive shit. But I was jealous. I wanted to tell Nate to back the fuck off. She was mine.

That would be a little too caveman for her and she would kick me to the curb right alongside Nate.

Chapter Fifteen

Bree

I WAS SO EXCITED, SO tired of being stuck in the house. I couldn't wait to go somewhere new. This trip was my getaway—my prison break. I planned on taking advantage of every minute of it. My dad had tried to talk me out of it again last night, but I was not going to be swayed. Life was short. I had learned that the hard way and didn't plan on leaving this earth without living as much as I could.

"You good?" Luke asked, leaning into me.

I smiled, nodding my head. I was wearing my sunglasses on the plane. The light from the windows was just enough to make me squint. "I'm so good. I know we just took a flight, but this feels like the first time in a very long time. I also know it isn't a vacation and the trip won't be a blast, but I am excited to see something new."

"Hopefully, we'll get there, and all will be well. We can spend a couple days seeing the city if you like."

"I would love that, but please don't think you have to entertain me. I came along to support you and I will be just fine."

"Thanks."

When we touched down in Dallas, I immediately felt the difference in the climate. It was warm and sticky. Luke never let go of my hand as we navigated the busy airport. I could feel my anxiety ramping up with the crush of people going to and from, and being unable to see them clearly. Luke picked up the rental car he had reserved and quickly ushered me into the car.

"How are you doing?" he asked.

I blew out a breath. "That was kind of intense."

"I'm sorry."

"Don't be. I have to get familiar with these things again. I've been alone and cooped up in that house for so long, I've forgotten what it's like to be in a crowd."

"I'm sure it isn't easy when you can't see well," he said.

"No, but so much better than blind, plus having you there next to me certainly makes it easier to tolerate."

I tried to look out the window, but everything was a blur. I could see the outline of tall buildings and the movement of cars going past the window, but not much more than that. When the car came to a stop, I looked out the window, trying to see the house.

"We'll check in and get settled before we go to the hospital," he said.

"Check in?" I questioned.

"Check into our room. I hope it's okay that I only got one room."

"Yes, it's fine. I just assumed we would be staying at your mom's house."

He made a choking sound. "No. I don't want to be there, and trust me, you don't want to be there either."

I didn't know what that meant but it didn't sound good. "Hotel it is."

He grabbed both our suitcases, before I hooked my arm through his and let him lead the way. I could hear the sound of a waterfall and was curious to see where it was coming from. I took off my glasses, squinting against the bright sun streaming through the windows in the ceiling. It took a few seconds for my eyes to adjust, but in the center of the lobby, I could make out the source of the water. It was a huge fountain.

It was a nice hotel. An expensive hotel. I had a feeling he had re-served a room in a more expensive hotel because of me. "I would have been okay at your mom's house," I said as we walked to the elevators.

"No, you wouldn't have, and neither would I."

"What's wrong with it?"

He sighed, shaking his head. "She isn't the best housekeeper. She says she is too sick to clean. I used to go to her place twice a week just to clean. I doubt she has cleaned up and I doubt she has paid anyone else to do it."

"Oh," I said, suddenly very glad he got the hotel. "Can I pay for the hotel at least?" I asked.

"No," his answer was firm. "This is my trip. We're here because of my mother. I'll pay."

"Can I buy dinner?"

He laughed. "Damn, you are persistent."

"Yes, I am. Please, let me treat you to at least one dinner while we are here. You have done so much for me. I want to thank you. I would never get to leave the house if it wasn't for you."

"We'll see," he answered before steering me into the elevator.

We got to our room, which was thankfully very modest. I would have felt horribly guilty if he had gotten us an expensive suite. I could make out the bed in the middle of the room and the row of windows. I immediately went to the windows and opened the curtains. I needed a bit more light to really see anything.

"This is nice," I commented.

"I know you are probably used to something a little more upscale, but I wasn't planning on being here for long."

Frowning, I turned to look at him. I put my hands on my hips to let him know I was very serious. "Luke Turner, don't you dare make me sound like a snob! I am not like that. I am very happy with the accommodations and I will not be insulted like that."

"I'm sorry," he blurted out as he walked towards me. "I didn't mean to sound like a dick. It was more self-deprecating than an insult towards you. You are wealthy. I'm not. It's something that feels very weird to me."

"Don't feel weird. I don't care about your wealth or lack thereof. I care about you. Money doesn't matter to me. We could be in a tiny little motel and I would be okay with it."

He laughed. "Really?"

I wrinkled my nose. "Okay, maybe it would be a little icky, but I would be fine."

He grinned and pulled me into his arms. "I'm sorry if I hurt your feelings. You are the most humble rich woman I know."

I smirked. "And I suppose I'm the only one you know."

"I know Mel," he countered.

"Two. You know two."

"And you win most humble," he teased.

"You're such a smooth talker," I said with a laugh.

"You haven't seen anything yet. Are you ready to do this?"

I reached up to touch my hand to his face. It was our thing. For so long I couldn't see him and always touched his face to make sure I was at least facing him when I talked. It was a habit. "I think the real question is; are you?"

He hesitated, which told me he wasn't ready. "Yes," he finally answered. "We've come all this way. Sitting in the hotel room isn't going to make it go away or make it any easier."

"Then, let's do this."

I put on my sunglasses and allowed him to lead me out of the hotel. We were fairly close to the hospital apparently. Fifteen minutes later, we were in a parking garage and the sunglasses were no longer needed.

He took my hand in his and led the way. "Are you doing okay?" he asked, when the sound of a siren in the distance cut through the air.

I nodded, putting on my sunglasses before we walked into the hospital. "It is strange, but I don't feel that same panic that I used to."

"Good. We're going to go inside. Are you ready?"

I smiled at him. "I am." I loved that he checked in with me, always taking my temperature so to speak. It was part of his caring nature.

"Hey, it's Nurse McHottie," I heard someone say.

I turned towards the female voice, ready to attack. I heard Luke laugh. His hand dropped mine and through my hazy vision, I could see him hugging a female. An older female judging by the roundness of the figure and the voice. My claws retracted a bit.

"Hi Helen," Luke greeted. "I've missed you. How are the kids?"

"They are devils," she replied. "I heard about your mama, honey. I'm sorry."

"Hey, it's okay," Luke replied. "I know she's in good hands."

"The best," Helen said.

He introduced me as his friend before we headed down a long, wide hall to the elevators. I wasn't offended that he referred to me as his friend. Technically, I was his friend. We weren't officially dating. We were stopped twice more before we made it to his mother's room. It was pretty clear we were in the hospital he worked at before he moved to California.

"In here," he said, in a quiet voice.

I was suddenly nervous. Memories of her snarky comments washed over me. She didn't like me. I knew that and I told myself I didn't care, but I did. I knew Luke cared about her and I wanted to try and make her like me.

"Mom," he whispered.

The room was dim, and I wondered if she was sleeping. I didn't take off my sunglasses. They acted as a security blanket, like my shield against her venom.

"Luke," I heard a weak voice. "Is that you?"

He gave my hand a squeeze before releasing it. "It's me," he said. "How are you feeling?"

"I'm dying," she answered.

That sounded a little dire. I didn't know any dying people that actually said they were dying. "I talked with your doctor last night and he said you are responding well to the treatment."

"He's a liar!" she snapped. "I'm in pain."

There was a silence. "Mom, with the amount of morphine flowing through your veins, it's a miracle you can even talk."

I knew that tone. It was his clinical voice. "You don't know what I feel," she whined.

"I'm looking at your morphine drip. It's high. Most people would be out cold. You have a very high tolerance for these meds."

Then I understood his tone. He was irritated. "I'm still in pain," she shot back. "You don't understand. Maybe I could just go home. I think I could get better under your care. These other doctors and nurses just aren't that good. I need your care."

There was a knock on the door. I heard shuffling footsteps and turned to see a man in a white coat. "Luke, it's good to see you. How is California treating you?"

"Good," Luke answered. "Are you doing the dialysis today?"

"I'm just checking some labs," the man answered.

I took a tentative step back, feeling very in the way. I listened to Luke and the doctor spoke. They were speaking in a foreign language as far as I was concerned. Soon, the doctor left, and it was just the three of us again.

"I suppose you can't take care of me because you have your other patient with you," Charlene said after the doctor left.

I tried to remember she wasn't well, and she was sick. She was lashing out.

"Mom, don't start," Luke said with obvious exasperation. "Bree is here as my friend."

"I'm not a zoo animal to be gawked at by your friends," she said.

"She isn't gawking at you, Mom. She's blind, remember."

I looked at him, wondering why he said that. I didn't question it just then. He had to have his reasons.

"You know what I mean," she complained.

I wanted to shrink into the size of a pea. I felt completely out of place. Luke was beside me in a second, his hand taking mine. "I need her here," he said.

I smiled up at him. "Thank you," I whispered.

He squeezed my hand, reassuring me it was going to be okay. I hoped so. I was beginning to regret coming along for the ride.

Chapter Sixteen

Luke

I NEEDED TO TALK WITH the patient care coordinator. I didn't like what I was seeing. I was tempted to see if my old log in information would work so I could look at her file. I wanted the whole picture. I looked at Bree who looked very uncomfortable. I shouldn't have brought her to the hospital. I knew my mother couldn't be trusted to behave herself.

"Mom, we are going to go grab a cup of coffee," I said, looking for an excuse to go in search of someone who could give me some answers.

"I'm okay," Bree whispered.

"You can't stand to be in the same room with me," my mother pouted.

I ignored her. It was moments like these I wished Bree could see my face. I would be able to tell her without words that I wanted to leave the room for a minute. I gave her hand a gentle squeeze and then tugged. "I could use some coffee," I said again.

She must have understood. "Me too."

"Fine. Leave me alone."

"We'll be back in a bit mom, try and sleep," I ordered.

I walked out of the room with Bree's hand in mine. "What's up?" she asked after we cleared the room.

"I want to talk to her doctor. Something isn't adding up."

"What do you mean?"

I shook my head. "She is suffering from kidney failure, but she is also claiming to be in a lot of pain. I saw an antibiotic hanging as well."

"Like she has an infection?" Bree asked.

"Yes. There is a bench right here. Will you be okay on your own for a few minutes?"

"Go ahead, I'm good," she said with a smile.

I patted her leg and walked to the nurse's station. I used my charm to get the doctor to meet me in person to discuss my mother's situation. I went back to Bree. "The doctor is going to meet with me to go over my mom's case. We'll need to go downstairs."

"I can wait here," she said. "I don't want to intrude."

"You are not intruding," I insisted.

"This is probably private," she said. "Can you take me to the waiting room?"

"Do you want to stay up here or downstairs?"

She laughed. "I'm going to leave that to your discretion. You know this hospital. Put me somewhere I won't be in the way."

"You are never in the way," I told her. "I think you'll like the waiting room here. It's quieter and cleaner."

I led the way, grabbing her a soda and some chips from the vending machine before heading downstairs. I found the patient care coordinator's office and knocked on the door.

"Luke Turner?" an older woman said stepping forward.

"Yes."

"Have a seat. What kind of questions did you have?"

I cleared my throat. "I was hoping you could fill me in on what is happening. I see she's on morphine for pain, but isn't that counteractive to the kidney failure?"

"Yes, but your mother's kidney failure is a bit of an odd one. She complained of being in severe pain. As you know, that isn't exactly common. Her symptoms vary by the day. The morphine is what has kept her comfortable."

I nodded. "She asked for it," I said, already knowing the truth.

"We did try other options, but she didn't get the desired pain relief."

I bit my tongue. Of course not. She liked morphine. She always had. I didn't think she was an addict, but she did enjoy a good numbing. Or maybe she was an addict. Something was wrong, but nobody had any clue what. "And the antibiotic?"

"Your mother had a nasty pressure sore that was horribly infected."

"What?" I asked with shock. "She isn't bedridden?"

The woman shrugged. "I can't answer that. Your mother is not getting the care she needs."

"She's not an invalid!" I argued, hating that word and hating myself for using it. I was on the defensive. I felt like it was my fault. "I don't understand this."

"She's going to need to long-term care," she said.

I didn't need to hear anymore. I firmly believed my mother had done it to herself. She had purposely made herself sick. The pressure sore was of her own doing. She had flown out to California on her own. She was not a person with physical disabilities. Whatever this was, she had done it to herself.

"Thank you for taking the time to meet with me," I said. I got to my feet. "I'm going to go back up."

"We can talk about next steps," she said with a smile.

"Thanks. I'll let you know."

I walked out and headed back upstairs. I was pissed. And scared. My mother was desperate. Desperate enough to do something that could have killed her. I couldn't understand it. I knew there was no explaining mental illness, but it just felt like I should understand it better. She was my mother. We shared the same blood. I didn't feel like I was like her in any way. I felt normal. What went wrong with her?

There was no point in trying to figure it out. I walked into the waiting room and saw Bree chatting with a little girl. Her sunglasses were off, and she looked stunning. The two were talking about a doll the little girl was holding. I watched them for a few minutes. Bree looked up and I saw the moment she recognized me. That was a bit of a surprise. Her blurred vision usually kept her from recognizing me until I was much closer.

"Hi," she said, smiling at me.

"Hi."

"All done?" she asked.

"Yes. Ready to go back in?"

Her smile never faltered. "I am."

If I was her, I would have said hell no and run the other way. Not Bree. She got up and came to me, reaching out to take my hand. We walked back to my mother's room, pushing open the door and finding her sitting up in bed and looking right as rain. Until she saw me. Then she was suddenly moaning and wincing.

"Did you enjoy your coffee?" she asked.

"Yes," I answered. "I spoke with your team," I started.

"I told you I was dying. What did they say? How long do I have?"

"You're not dying," I told her. "How did you get a bed sore?" I asked.

I heard Bree's sharp intake of breath, but kept my gaze focused on my mom, wanting to judge her reaction. "I was so sick," she moaned. "I couldn't get out of bed. I called you. I told you I was ill. I told you I was weak."

"You were too weak to roll over?" I snapped.

"Don't be so mean," she whimpered. "I'm suffering."

"Why are you on morphine?" I asked. "You should be fine with something milder. The doctors said you insisted."

"It's all that helps. Even now I'm in pain, but I'm trying to be a real trooper. I'm pushing through."

Rolling my eyes, I said, "You need to rest. There is nothing truly wrong with you."

"Look at these machines! I'm not faking it."

I shrugged. "No, but you can help yourself get better. You need to do what the doctors tell you. Quit trying to fight them and stop trying to tell them you know better. They know what they are doing. I want you to get better."

That last bit seemed to appease her a bit. There was a hint of a smile. "I'll try son. For you, I'll try."

"Good. Now, we're going to get out of here and give you some time to rest. Please, shut off the TV and get some sleep."

"You're leaving?" she gasped. "You just got here."

"I'll be back in the morning. You're in good hands."

"But I need you," she pleaded.

I shook my head. "No, you need rest and medicine. That's what you are getting here."

She didn't look happy. "Fine. I guess if I take a turn for the worse, someone can call you."

"You'll be fine, Mom. Goodnight." I walked over and gave her a kiss on the cheek before walking back to Bree and taking her hand.

We made it outside before I finally let released the breath I'd been holding.

"Are you okay?" Bree asked.

"I am."

"Are you sure? You don't have to entertain me. I can go back to the hotel and hang out."

"I was thinking we could do some sightseeing."

"Really?"

"Really," I said with a smile. "I'd love to show you around."

"Okay, I'm not going to argue with that. I would love to do some exploring."

"How is your sight?" I asked.

She grinned. "You know, I think it is actually getting better. We might have to fly again just to see if that's what did the trick."

I laughed. "I seriously doubt that was it, but I'm happy for you. Would you like to check out the Irving Art Center?"

She stopped walking, pulling me to a stop. "Seriously?"

"Absolutely. If you aren't too tired, we can head over to Fair Park."

"I won't be too tired," she said with excitement. "This is so awesome. Thank you."

Putting my arm around her, I hugged her close. "My pleasure."

We spent the rest of the afternoon doing the sightseeing she always said she wanted to do. I wished she could see the art better, but even with her blurred vision, she was thrilled. I couldn't wait to see how excited she would get when she could see art with clear eyes again.

"Are you hungry?" I asked.

"I'm famished," she said with a laugh.

"I know a place. You will get the best steak in all of Texas."

She laughed again. "I love a good steak. I think I might be able to see it well enough to cut it myself, too."

"I'm happy to cut it for you."

I took her to one of my favorite restaurants in the city. It wasn't a five-star restaurant, but it served some of the best food in the city. It had always been my go-to place for a first date. I hoped it was as good as the steakhouse she loved back home. I couldn't afford the prices there. I'd checked. Only one of us would be eating if I tried to take her there.

We sipped a delicious red wine while we dined on our appetizers. "So, what made you think your mom purposely gave herself a bed sore?" she asked.

I shrugged. "Because there is no medical reason for her to develop one. She's capable of walking, turning, and sitting up. She knows how to prevent them."

"Is it something she has done before?" she questioned.

I didn't want to ruin our perfect day and what I'd hoped would be a perfect meal by talking about my mother. "Not with bedsores, but yes, there have been other issues," I answered. "Did you have fun today?" I asked, changing the subject.

"I did. It was good. I'm definitely coming back as soon as my eyes are better. I want to see all that art better. Then, I want to go that farmer's market and look for pieces to put in the gallery I'm going to open."

She sounded so happy and enthusiastic, I couldn't help but smile. "We'll definitely come back. I can't say I've ever really paid attention to the art, but I know there are plenty of folks looking for their big break."

"I am looking forward to finding the diamond in the rough."

"And I am confident you will," I told her.

"Did you grow up in the city or in one of the smaller towns nearby?" she asked.

She was steering the conversation back to my past, and I just couldn't do it. I didn't want to talk about any of it. I didn't want to ruin the day. "I grew up nearby." I paused, then continued, "Listen Bree, I don't want to be a dick, but would you mind if we didn't talk about any of that right now? One day we will, but not today, okay?"

She looked disappointed but nodded. "Got it. No discussion about your childhood or anything personal."

The way she said it revealed her hurt. "It's just a long, sordid history and I really want to enjoy this dinner and spending time with you. Okay?"

She smiled. "Okay, but one day."

I grimaced. "One day," I grudgingly agreed, hoping that day never came. I would prefer to just move on and pretend none of it existed.

Chapter Seventeen

Bree

IT HAD BEEN THE BEST day and evening I'd had in a very long time. I felt good. Luke's hand held mine as we strolled along the sidewalk that led to our hotel. I could see the many lights from various buildings and businesses. I loved a city at night. While I knew it could be a little scary and dangerous, there was something extremely romantic about the lights and the stars above.

"How are you feeling?" Luke asked.

"Good. Excited for the future. Thank you for today. I wasn't expecting to have so much fun on this trip. You have blown my mind."

His soft, deep laughter warmed my soul. "I'm glad you are enjoying yourself. I'm glad I got to show you things you've never experienced, and I want to thank you for helping me see the city through a more positive perspective. It really is a wonderful place."

"I'm so glad you feel that way. I hope we can come back for regular visits. I'm sure your mom will appreciate that as well."

"More than you can ever know," he said in a somber tone.

We headed back to our room. I was riding high on good wine and a great day and didn't want the night to end. I kicked off my shoes and sank my feet into the fluffy carpet. I walked to the balcony and stepped outside, inhaling the night air. I could see the millions of lights twinkling around us.

A few minutes later, Luke joined me on the balcony. "Here," he said, touching my hand with a plastic cup.

I grinned. "I've never actually had wine from a plastic cup."

He laughed. "So, here's to new things. It's maybe a little redneck, but I promise you, it tastes the same."

Sipping from the glass, I smiled. "It sure does."

We stood in silence, enjoying spending time together just winding down from our busy day. It had been a full day. Especially considering the reality that the most active I had been in the last few months was hanging out at the beach for a couple hours. This day was a glimpse into my old life when I would hit the ground running every morning and not stop until around midnight.

"I think I'm going to change," I told him after I finished my wine.

"Need any help?" he offered.

I laughed. "Are you asking to take off my clothes?"

"Maybe," he teased.

"In that case, then yes, absolutely."

We walked into the room and instead of waiting for him to help me, I stepped out of the shorts I was wearing. I pulled off my shirt and stood there, waiting for him to finish closing the curtains. When he turned around, I was there, ready and waiting for him. "You're fast."

"You're a little too slow."

He chuckled and in a flurry of movement, his clothes were shed as well. He stepped towards me, his fingertips running down my arm before I felt him unhook my bra. He finished taking off the remainder of my clothing, leaving me naked and exposed to his gaze.

"You are absolutely gorgeous," he whispered, walking around me. I could feel the brush of his skin as he moved with his hand trailing a line over my waist, down to my butt and then back around to my belly. "Every inch of you is magnificent."

Goosebumps covered my body. His lips were soft as he kissed the side of my neck and then moved over my collar bone. It was sweet and gentle and was doing things to my body I couldn't quite explain. I shuddered as his tongue lapped out. He bent lower, his mouth covering one breast, then the next. My hands reached into his hair, gently pulling him closer, demanding more of the sensual kisses.

The kisses intensified, covering my upper body. He stepped close to me, his chest rubbing against mine as he backed me up. I felt the bed hit my legs followed by him lifting me up as if I weighed nothing. He deposited me on the bed, leaning over to kiss me until I felt I would erupt into flames.

He began another ridiculously hot trail of kisses over my shoulder and then between my breasts. I closed my eyes, blocking out the blurred images that my brain was trying to focus on. I didn't want to see anything in that moment. I only wanted to feel.

His kisses continued over my belly, landing right over my heated core. I cried out with the first contact. His tongue lapped over me, sending me into a tailspin of excitement and ecstasy. My hands gripped the comforter, holding on as my heels dug into the mattress. His magical mouth and tongue worked me into a frenzy until I was crying out with sheer pleasure.

The sensations made me feel like I was spinning into space before his heavy body settled over mine, grounding me once again. He was soon joining his body with mine, stretching me as he pushed deep inside. "You taste so good," he whispered next to my ear.

I groaned as he slowly moved inside me. "I love having you inside me. I love being with you."

He kissed my neck, taking his sweet time as he moved in and out of my body. "I can't get enough of you," he rasped. "Every time I look at you, I want to rip your clothes off and bury myself inside you. You make me feel like I will go crazy if I can't have you."

A languid smile spread over my face. "You can have me. Here I am. Take me."

He began to move faster, his need stealing away that smooth, gentle flow he had going. He suddenly pulled out of me. His hands were on my hips, frantically tugging and pulling. "Over. Get on your knees."

The demand in his voice sent a fresh wave of ecstasy over me. He sounded so, feral. So, unlike the gentle Luke I knew him to be. I quickly scrambled to do what he asked. One of his strong hands gripped my hip and the other guided himself to my center. With one hard thrust, he plunged inside me.

A cry escaped my lips. The force of his need excited me. My calm, cool Luke was gone and in his place was a man intent on pleasure. He growled, sounding downright ferocious as he rocked his body against mine. His heavy breathing combined with the grunts and growls turned me on. I loved that it was me who stripped away that cool veneer. I love that he was losing control because I turned him on that much.

I got into the spirit and pushed back, demanding more of him. He did not disappoint. He rocked harder and faster, nearly sending me headfirst into the wall. I dug in, pushing back and giving as hard as I was taking.

"Fuck," he groaned, his fingertips digging into my flesh as he moved faster.

I rotated my hips, scraping over the cock buried inside me. It was the trigger we both needed. I felt him jerk once, his body going completely stiff. His climax set off a series of fireworks inside me that started in the tips of my toes and rolled over my body. When my arms would no longer support me, I dropped face first onto the mattress. His heavy weight came down on me. He didn't move for several seconds.

"You okay?" he asked, moving off me, his hand stroking the hair that was clinging to my brow.

I smiled. "Oh, so much better than okay."

I rolled to my side, facing him. He was on his side as well, our faces merely inches apart. I could make out some of his features and with my imagination, I filled in the blanks about what I couldn't see. "What are you looking at?" he asked.

"You."

"Can you see me?"

"You're pretty damn close to my face, yes, I can see you."

He laughed. "You know what I mean? I'm looking into your eyes and it feels like you are looking directly into my soul."

"Maybe I am. I know you have blue eyes. I can't really see the color, but I see dark brows." I reached up and gently ran my fingertip over them.

"I have something for you. I was going to wait to give it to you, but I think you are ready for it."

I giggled. "I think I just had it, but I could be ready again."

He slapped my hip as he got up. "Get your mind out of the gutter."

"You say that and then you parade around a lighted room completely nude. What else am I supposed to think?"

He chuckled again before rejoining me on the bed. I rolled over, propping myself up against the tufted headboard. He held something out. "I got this for you."

"Is it a book?" I asked looking at the rectangular shape.

"No. It's a sketch pad."

Reaching out for it I grabbed it and pulled it to me. "Oh my gosh! I haven't sketched in forever."

"I got you some charcoal and an assortment of pencils. I wasn't sure what you preferred."

"Luke, this is awesome!"

"I was going to wait until your vision was better, but you are so talented, I'm not sure you really have to see. I bet you could truly draw with your eyes closed."

"Let's see," I said. "Can you hand me one of those pencils?"

He got off the bed again and was back in a flash. He put a pencil in my hand. I sat, cross-legged on the bed with the sketch pad opened. I didn't care that I was naked. It felt natural and safe to be like that with him.

I held the pencil in my hand over the paper and waited for inspiration to come. I began with light strokes. The black on white was easier for me to see. My hand flew over the paper. It really was like riding a bike. I could see the imagine coming alive on the paper and in my imagination.

When I was finished, I stared down at the strokes. While they didn't necessarily form a cohesive picture to my eyes, I hoped they did for his.

"Can I see?" he asked.

I turned the sketchpad towards him. "It could be a masterpiece, or it could look like a toddler got their hands on a black crayon."

"It's me," he said with surprise. "Holy shit. How did you do that?"

"Does it really look like you?" I asked hopefully.

"Yes. Oh my goodness, Bree. I'm blown away. It's awesome. I can't believe you just did that. You have real talent, Bree. Even if your sight doesn't come back all the way, you don't need it."

I smiled. "Maybe not, but I would like it all the same."

He pulled me in for a hug. "I would like you to have it as well. Are you going to let me have that?"

"Maybe. I think I would like to work on it a little more first."

"You amaze me," he whispered before pulling me in for a kiss. I tossed the sketchpad and pencil on the floor.

"Let me show you some of the other ways I can amaze you," I whispered, pushing him onto his back.

Chapter Eighteen

Luke

I WOKE UP WITH BREE'S head resting on my chest. It was the best feeling in the world. I didn't move. I laid perfectly still and just listened to the sound of her breathing. There was nowhere else I wanted to be. Except maybe in California in my own place. Being with her was the best thing in the world. The way I felt for her was a little terrifying. She had my heart. Which meant she could break it.

It was frightening and I hated giving someone that much power, but I had to have faith that she wouldn't hurt me. I trusted her. I had a friend that always said you had to trust someone. I didn't buy into that logic, but I did now. I turned my head to look at the clock. We had slept in and it felt amazing.

I did want to get to the hospital and check on my mom. I wasn't convinced her condition was the result of any particular disease or illness. I wanted to see for myself what her labs looked like and what tests had been done. Honestly, I suspected she was making herself sick, but I had no idea how. I couldn't imagine anyone wanting to feel miserable, but my mother wasn't normal and I had to keep that in mind. One couldn't use typical logic to try and understand her.

Gently, I moved, trying to disentangle her body from mine without waking her. I wasn't successful.

"What time is it?" she asked.

"Almost nine."

"Oh my gosh! Seriously?"

"Yes. I was just getting up to hop in the shower. I was thinking, I would run over and check in on my mom and then we can spend the day together."

"You don't want me to go with you?"

Smiling, I rubbed her arm. "I would love to have you there, but my mom is just not nice and I don't want to subject you to her nastiness. Is that okay?"

"I get it, but I don't mind sitting in the waiting room while you visit with her."

"No, I can't ask you to do that," I insisted. "I'm hoping to get a look at some of her lab work, too, and would feel back leaving you to wait. You'll be more comfortable here."

"Okay. Maybe I'll just sketch and be a lazy bum."

"That would make you officially the hottest bum I've ever laid eyes on."

I gave her a kiss and climbed out of bed, naked as the day I was born. "I can see you," she said.

"Like all of me, or my blurry blob."

She laughed. "I can't see the hairs on your arm, or other parts, but I can see you. I can see your shape. It's kind of like looking in a foggy mirror, but it's better than it was even a few days ago."

"I'm so happy for you. You're going to be seeing perfectly in a day or two, I just know it. Wear your sunglasses if you open those curtains."

"Yes, sir."

Smiling, I walked into the bathroom. I had a feeling part of her new sight was more of a mental thing. She was free of the stress of being back home. She was in a new place and she wanted to see. It was mind over matter and she was practically healing herself. I left her with the room service menu, which she couldn't read, but she said she would figure it out.

When I got to the hospital, I caught the team of doctors just as they were finishing their rounds in my mother's room.

"There he is!" my mother exclaimed.

"Ah, I do remember him," one of the doctors said.

I couldn't remember the guy's name. It was a big hospital and most of my time had been spent downstairs in the emergency department. "Luke Turner," I said, and extended my hand.

"I'm Dr. Prince and these are my interns. We were just chatting with your mother about her long-term care outlook."

I nodded. "And?"

"We've seen improvements. Her kidney function is improving, and her levels are evening out a bit. We're ready to drop her down to twice a week dialysis with the goal of weaning her off."

"That is good news."

"She would like to go home," the doctor said.

"So, she has said," I said, nodding.

"I don't see any reason she can't be sent home. I understand you are a registered nurse and were her caregiver for quite some time. I'm comfortable releasing her into your care. We find a lot of patients tend to get better faster when they are in the comfort of their own home."

It was an ambush. I looked to my mother and saw her faint smile. She was setting me up. I would look like an asshole if I said I couldn't take care of her.

"Did she tell you I live out of state?" I asked.

Dr. Prince looked surprised. "No, she didn't. How long are you in town for?"

I shrugged. "I flew in to see how she was doing. She appears to be in good care."

Call me an asshole.

"I see," he said. "She would need care and if there isn't someone there to make sure she is getting meds and monitoring her vitals, I don't think it's a good idea to release her."

"You'll stay, won't you son? You know how much I hate hospitals. I don't want to be a burden, but I just don't think I'll get better here."

I looked to the doctors who were all staring at me like I was the worst human being on the planet. I offered a small smile. "We'll talk about it. I do have obligations in California that I need to consider."

My mother waved a hand. "I'm sure she'll be fine. Her father can afford to hire twenty nurses. She doesn't need you. I do. I need my son to see me through this dark time."

I shot her a look. I didn't need my dirty laundry aired for the entire hospital. "We'll talk it over," I said again.

"I'll be by tomorrow," Dr. Prince said, before walking out with the other two interns behind him.

"Where's your little girlfriend," my mother asked.

"Don't do that, Mother. Don't be rude. She's never done anything to you."

"She took you away from me."

"No, she didn't. I'm still your son."

She sighed, picking at invisible lint on the blanket. "You know what I mean. You don't want to help me get better because you are too caught up with her."

"That isn't true, Mom. I do want you to get better."

I moved to sit in the chair beside the bed. The relationship I had with my mother was something I couldn't quite explain. I loved her, but I hated who she was. I hated that she just couldn't be a normal mom. I hated that we couldn't have a normal relationship. I missed the early days, the good days. The last few years, there had been very few good days. The older she got, the worse things had been.

"I know I could get better if I had you taking care of me. You always take such good care of me."

"You have to want to get better," I told her.

Even as I sat there, I could feel my defenses slipping. My natural instinct was to be there for her. I wanted her to get better. I hated the idea of anyone being sick. I loved her and I could see she was suffering, even if it was exaggerated or self-induced. The dialysis was no joke.

"I do, I swear I do. I've never been this sick before."

"No, you haven't," I agreed. "You have to take better care of yourself."

"I know and I will, but I just need you to help me through this. I swear, I will do better."

I wanted to believe her. Part of me did believe her. Maybe it was what she needed to be scared straight. She had come very close to dying and I couldn't help but feel guilty about that. She had called numerous times and told me this was different, but I didn't buy it.

"Are you still going to that book club?" I asked.

She shrugged. "Not really. Those ladies are stuck up."

"Mom, you used to like them."

"They treat me like I'm trash," she said.

My mom thought everyone treated her like trash. I used to believe it, then I witnessed someone treating her like trash. Basically, they didn't dote on her, which in her mind, meant they hated her. Just like Bree. "I think you need to make some friends," I told her. "You used to have some good friends. Part of staying healthy is staying happy. If you let yourself get down, you're going to get sick."

She let out a sigh. "I know, I've just been so sad with you gone."

"Mom, I am enjoying my life out there. Can't you be happy for me?"

"But why there? It's so far away?"

Because it's so far away.

"It's a nice place to live and I'm exploring my options right now. I need to live my life."

She was quiet for a few seconds. "I know. It's just so hard not having you around."

She was being normal. The things she was saying weren't too over the top. She was lonely. I could understand that. I had treated many elderly patients in the Emergency Department that were lonely. They let themselves go and landed in one of our beds. They just needed a little attention. My mother was no different.

"I need to make a call," I said, after we had spent an hour together.

"Are you coming back?" she asked.

"Yes. Just give me a few minutes."

I walked down the hall, and stepped into the waiting room that was thankfully empty. I called Bree.

"Hey," she answered. "How's it going?"

"Good," I said, feeling horrible about what I was about to do. "I think I'm going to need to stay here for a while."

"Okay," she quickly answered. "Be with your mom. I'm totally fine here. I'm enjoying the peace and doing some sketching. I might go down to the pool later."

"Bree, you can't swim yet," I lectured.

She laughed. "I know. I was just going to lay out."

"In one of those sexy bikinis?" I asked in a husky voice.

"Maybe," she teased.

"You're killing me."

"I'm sorry. How is she?"

I sighed. "She seems to be doing a little better. I'm just going to stay with her for a while. We can catch an early dinner if that's okay?"

"Of course, it's okay. You're here to see your mother, not to hang out with me. I really am okay on my own."

"Thank you," I said, feeling grateful to have a woman that was so understanding.

"You're welcome. Take care of her and make sure you take care of yourself."

I smiled. "I will."

"I would ask you to tell her I said hi, but I'm guessing that wouldn't be helpful," she said with a laugh.

"I'm sorry," I apologized. "She can be a real bear when she isn't feeling well. Or any time, for that matter. Don't take it personally. It's just her being her."

"I'm not. I'll talk to you soon."

Ending the call, I felt a lot less guilty about standing her up. I could almost feel my heart being torn in two. The guilt I felt on both sides was killing me. I felt guilty for leaving my mother and sending her into this latest bout of sickness. I felt guilty for leaving Bree stranded and alone in a strange place without the ability to see.

This guilt was crushing. I told myself I would hang out with my mom, give her the attention she needed, then rush back to the hotel to give Bree some attention as well. I could do it. It was the only way I was going to be able to live with myself.

Chapter Nineteen

Bree

I WASN'T BORED, WHICH kind of surprised me. I had made my way down to the poolside and spent a couple hours soaking up the Texas sun. And for the first time in a very long time, I felt truly independent. Six months ago, hanging out poolside by myself would have been no big deal. I would have complained about being alone or being bored. Now, it felt like I was getting to take the car out for the first time by myself.

Honestly, what I felt was free. I couldn't see a hundred percent, but I could see enough to keep me from falling into the pool or ramming my face into a wall. For the first time in months, I was doing whatever the hell I felt like. No one was telling me to watch out. I felt alive. I felt like the old me. I was Bree two-point-o.

Luke had sounded worried, like I would be upset that he was spending the day with his mom. I wasn't. Not in the slightest. He needed to be with her. She needed him. Just then, I did not need him. Wanting him, enjoyed him, yes to both. But need him, no. I liked that I could be okay and let him do his thing. Slowly, I was beginning to feel like the other half in our relationship. For too long, he had carried the full weight. I wanted him to need me. I wanted him to lean on me just a little.

After changing into a pair of shorts and one of the new shirts I bought on my little shopping spree, I decided to brave going out on my own. I wasn't going to go far. I knew there was a little coffee shop next to the hotel. I wouldn't have to cross the street and risk getting flattened by a truck.

Following my nose, the scent of rich coffee was a beacon to my senses. I managed to order and pay without making a complete fool of myself. With my coffee in hand, I made my way back to the hotel and up to our room. Once inside the room, I let out a whoop of glee. "I did it!" I squealed.

It was my first solo mission in months. It felt like years. I couldn't wait to call Mel and tell her. I couldn't wait to tell Luke! My dad would not be nearly as thrilled with the idea. I took off the sunglasses, letting my eyes adjust to the room with the filtered sunlight coming in through the sheer curtains.

Grabbing my phone, I called Mel. "Guess what I just did!" I said when she picked up.

"If you say Luke, I'm hanging up."

Laughing, I replied smugly. "No. Actually I did that last night," I teased. "No, I went and got coffee all by myself!"

"Wow! Look at you go, Miss Independent!"

I laughed, taking a sip of the coffee I had procured all by myself. "I cannot believe I'm celebrating getting coffee, but seriously, this is amazing."

"Where is Luke?" she asked.

"He's at the hospital with his mom. They needed some time. Not to mention, the woman hates me. I don't want to make her sicker by being nearby."

"Why does she hate you?" she asked.

I shrugged. "Because I'm rich. Because her son lives in California. Because I'm with her son in California."

She laughed. "That sounds pretty typical. Does this mean your sight is back?"

"It's getting there. The blobs I see have more defined shapes now. I can make out doors and if I move slow, I won't run anyone over."

"That is awesome! I am so happy for you. How long do you think you will be in Dallas?"

I sighed. "I'm not sure. He is trying to understand what happened. Yesterday, we went to a gallery and explored the city. It was amazing. I had so much fun. I felt a little guilty, treating the trip like a vacation, considering the fact that we are here because his mom is deathly ill, though."

"You are still allowed to have fun," she pointed out.

"Thank you. I did."

We chatted a bit more before she had to go. I put on my sunglasses and stepped out onto the tiny balcony. It was a warm day, but not uncomfortable. I put my feet up on the railing, crossed at the ankles and enjoyed the sounds of the busy city floating up from below.

My phone rang, disturbing my quiet reflection. I assumed it was Luke and quickly answered. "Hello?"

"Bree?" I heard a man's voice say.

I sat forward, putting my feet on the floor. The voice was familiar, but I couldn't quite place it. "This is she."

"This is Anton Burnett," he said.

My mind did a quick memory bank search. The name registered and I jumped to my feet. "Anton! Oh my gosh. Are you back in the States?"

He chuckled. "I am. I get home only to find you have flown the state!"

"I'm just in Texas for a few days. How are you? How were your travels?"

"Good. Great. I spoke with Nate and he told me about the accident. I'm so sorry to hear you had to go through that. All is well now?"

I sighed. "It's getting there. I hope to be fully recovered in a few weeks."

"Good to hear. Nate also mentioned you were talking about the gallery idea. Is that still something you want to do?"

"Yes!" I practically shouted the world. "It is. I'm hoping to start looking for a location once my sight is better."

"What if I told you I had the perfect place. It's a little small, but I think it may be perfect for what you have in mind, assuming you are still talking about that farfetched idea we hatched out over one too many margaritas a few years ago."

I laughed. "It's not so farfetched. I thought you were opening a gallery in Paris or something like that?"

"I did and it is a huge success, which is why I am back here. I was hoping we could talk about a partnership."

My head was spinning. "Did Nate put you up to this?" I asked.

Anton chuckled. "Absolutely not. I never got the impression that Nate was thrilled with the idea. I asked him if you were interested and he reluctantly told me yes. I got the feeling he was more on board with the idea this time around than the first time we talked about it, though."

"Did Nate tell you we weren't together?" I questioned.

"He did, but he said you two were still great friends."

Great friends was a bit of an exaggeration, but I was happy he was willing to support the idea. He had always been adamantly against it in the past. Maybe Nate had changed.

"Wow. I'm floored. I don't know what to say."

"Say we can meet for coffee and go over some of the details."

I grinned. There was no way in hell I was going to say no. "Can I call you tomorrow and let you know when I'll be back in town?"

"Sure."

"Are you going to be in town for a while?"

"I am. My gallery is in good hands over there, and I want to open one here."

"Look at you being all business-y," I teased.

"I am determined to prove to my father that there is money in art, even if it isn't my art that I'm selling," he laughed. "I will have to agree with him that my art was shit."

"It wasn't shit," I told him.

"You're lying and I love you for it. Call me when you get back into town."

"I will. Did you bring Tracy with you or leave her in Paris?"

"My lovely wife is still in Paris and will be coming home next week."

I smiled, thinking about the two of them together. They were a couple I envied. Their love for each other was so obvious. "I can't wait to see her. I'll call you soon and let you know when I'll be back."

"Take care," he said, and ended the call.

I had barely put the phone down when it rang again. I was suddenly feeling very popular. "Hello?"

"Hey there," Luke's deep voice washed over me.

"Hi."

"Are you bored?" he asked.

"Nope."

"Liar. Would you like to come hang out with us for a bit?"

"Sure," I quickly answered, happy he wanted me there.

"I'll come and pick you up. She's eating her lunch right now."

"Sounds good," I said.

I was anxious to tell him my news. I would wait until tonight when we were alone, though. I didn't want to give Charlene any more ammunition. She hated me enough already. If I sounded happy about my life in California, it was sure to make her hate me even more.

It wasn't long before Luke was coming through the door. He walked straight over and pulled me into his arms for a warm hug followed by a sensual kiss. "You make my heart pound," I told him.

He laughed. "You make me hard, so I guess we're even."

I giggled. "You're naughty."

"Ready?" he asked, clearly anxious to get back.

"I am."

As we walked to the elevator, I told him about my excursion to get coffee. "That was daring and I'm glad I didn't know you were doing it. I would have been completely stressed out."

Grinning, I nodded. "I know. But I was fine and it really felt great. How is your mom doing?"

"She seems a little better today."

"Good! I'm so happy to hear that."

We made it back to his mother's room. She was sitting in a chair watching TV and finishing up her lunch. "You're back," she said, in a tight voice.

"Hello Charlene," I said, with a friendly smile, hoping to disarm the woman.

"Bree, I need to talk to the nurse," Luke said. "Can you wait here?"

"Sure."

He guided me to another chair. I sat down, leaving my sunglasses on. Not because I needed them, but because I didn't want the woman looking directly into my eyes. She kind of freaked me out.

"How are you feeling?" I asked in a light tone.

I watched her wave a hand. She was testing me. She was trying to see if I could see her. I decided to play blind, wanting to see what she would do. I was expecting her to make faces or flip me off. When I had no reaction to the waving hand, she leaned over and grabbed what appeared to be a purse or a bag.

"I'm doing much better now that my son is here," she answered.

Watching, she rummaged around in the bag. A few seconds later, I heard the sound of pills being shaken out of a bottle and then she was taking a long drink. "I'm glad Luke was able to make it out here," I said, not letting on I had just watched her take something.

It could have been Advil for all I knew, or maybe some mints. I couldn't say for sure because I couldn't see clearly, which pissed me off. I held my smile. "He has always taken care of me," she went on. "He's a good boy."

"Yes, he is. He really loves California, though."

"He is a Texas boy. Our children must leave the nest and stretch their wings, but they always come back. I know he needs to explore, but he'll come back."

She sounded very confident of that fact. "Maybe one day he will," I agreed.

We both fell quiet. It was clear we had nothing in common except Luke and that was also the one thing we would never see eye to eye on. I sat with her for what felt like forever until Luke came back in.

Without warning, I heard Luke shout for help and then rush to his mother's side. There was a horrible beeping coming from the machine and a flurry of activity. I was afraid to move from my chair but felt in the way. I managed to stand and slide against the wall and make my way out of the room. I leaned against the wall in the hallway and waited for Luke to tell me what was going on.

Chapter Twenty

Luke

I STARED AT MY MOTHER lying in the hospital bed. She looked pale. The doctors had managed to get her stabilized after the episode. I looked at the nurse who was closely monitoring her vitals. During the chaotic ten minutes, I had been pushed out of the way. I found Bree outside the room and had gone back inside to see what was happening. Now that everyone had cleared out and my heart had slowed down, I could finally think straight.

"What happened?" I asked, for what felt like the hundredth time.

My mom's eyes fluttered open. "Luke?" she whispered my name.

"I'm here, Mom," I said, and took her hand in mine.

"The doctor has ordered more tests," the nurse answered. "For now, she seems stable. Her blood pressure is a little low, but we'll keep an eye on it. I'll check back in fifteen minutes."

I nodded as she walked out of the room. "Mom, can you tell me what happened? You were fine."

She slowly shook her head. "I don't know. I just got so dizzy and lightheaded. Then my heart was racing, and I was cold and hot."

I couldn't understand what had happened. I was just thinking we were in the clear and had been speaking with her doctor about getting her home or into a care facility. "Do you think it was something you ate?" I asked.

"I don't know, but I do feel like I'm going to throw up. Can you give me that basin?"

I quickly reached for it, holding it for her. She vomited the little lunch she had managed to get down. I sighed, realizing she was much sicker than I thought. "Better?" I asked taking away the basin and getting a washcloth for her.

She leaned back against the pillow. "Yes. But so drowsy."

"Get some sleep. I'm turning off the TV. You need to rest without that noise."

"Don't leave," she pouted.

It was like a being doused with ice water. The way she said it was eerily reminiscent of the many times in the past when she wanted to manipulate me into sticking around. I looked down at her. Her eyes were closed, and she did look like hell, but there was a soft smile on her lips. I didn't want to think it, but I had to wonder if I had just been duped.

Was she playing me? I shook my head. The incident had been very real. That couldn't have been faked. Regardless, I felt like she was sucking me into the old ways. I needed some air. I needed a minute to think without seeing her sickly face. "I'm going to get some lunch," I told her. "Try and sleep."

"Please come back. Don't leave me alone. I just can't be alone."

"You're not alone. You have a whole team of nurses around. If you need something, hit your call button."

She let out a heavy sigh. "Fine. Go eat. It isn't like I'll be going anywhere."

I told myself to be strong. I knew when she was working me and just then, she was working me. I walked out of the room and found Bree standing against the wall. The poor woman looked like she was trying to fade into the pastel blue paint on the walls.

"Hey," I said, as I touched her arm.

"How is she?" she asked with concern.

"She's okay now."

"How are you?" she asked, reaching up and gently touching my cheek.

I smiled. "Better now that I'm with you."

"Do you need anything?"

"I need a break from this," I told her.

"Why don't we go down to the cafeteria? Have you eaten anything?"

I shook my head. "No."

"Let's get you something to eat," she said, looping her arm through mine.

I let her lead me to the elevator. For a brief moment, I leaned on her. It felt good to have someone concerned for me. With a few simple words and her touch, I felt better, stronger. I could get through whatever it was coming my way.

We made it to the cafeteria. I wasn't really all that hungry, but I knew I needed to eat. We carried our salads to a table and sat down. The cafeteria was relatively empty with the lunch rush behind us. "What have you been up to?" I asked her.

She smiled. "I was proud of myself for going out to get coffee."

"Oh crap, I forgot about that. Where did you go, do I dare ask?"

"Next door to the hotel."

"Bree! You are... awfully proud of yourself, I see," I said, not sure if I was happy for her or terrified. But judging by the look on her face, she was very empowered and I wasn't going to tarnish that obvious victory with a scolding.

"I'm fine. It was fun. I felt so free."

"I'm glad you enjoyed yourself."

"There's something else," she said, with a huge grin on her face.

I was almost afraid to ask. "Don't tell me you rented a car and went for a drive," I teased.

She laughed. "No, not yet. I'm going to open a gallery!"

I didn't know what to say. "Today?"

"No silly. I've told you about this."

"I know but I didn't think you'd get it all figured out of a morning. I'm impressed. I leave you alone for a few hours and you're out conquering the world."

She laughed again. "I'm so excited. I feel like I'm getting my life back."

"Tell me about this gallery thing. Did you find a space or what?"

"Yes. Well, I didn't, my friend did."

"Mel?" I asked.

"No. Anton is he name. He's an old friend of Nate's that I met a few years ago. We shared an interest in art. He moved away a little over a year ago to open a gallery in Paris. He's back, talked to Nate and apparently found out I was still interested and long story short, we're going to do it together."

The woman was bubbling over with excitement. I could see how happy she was. She was elated. I was happy for her, but all I kept hearing was Nate. Nate's friend. It was her old life. Her connection to Nate was still there. "That's great," I forced myself to say.

She frowned. "I might not be able to see your expression, but I can hear it in your voice. You're not happy. If it's Anton you're worried about, no need. He is happily married to his beautiful wife Tracy, who I like very much."

"No," I quickly said. "I am so happy for you. This is what you have been talking about for weeks. I'm happy to hear it's coming true for you. You deserve it."

"But?" she pressed.

I sighed. "I'm happy for you. I really am. It's just this stuff with my mom has me spun up. Don't let me take away from your celebrating. I cannot wait to see what you do. I know you are going to have an awesome gallery."

She slowly nodded. "I'm sorry, Luke. You're dealing with a lot. I shouldn't be celebrating when you are dealing with something so serious."

"No, actually I'm happy for the distraction. This thing with my mom; I'm honestly not sure it's as serious as it may appear."

"What do you mean?"

I shook my head. "I don't know. It's hard to explain. I don't know if I'm just jaded, but it feels off."

Bree was staring down at the sandwich on her plate and I could see she had more to say. I was wondering what else she could have accomplished in the few short hours I had left her alone. Maybe she had found a house and her things were being moved as we spoke.

"Luke," she said, taking off her glasses and looking at me. I could see the trouble and uncertainty in her eyes.

"What is it?" I asked, knowing it wasn't good news she had to share. There was something wrong. I tried to tell myself not to jump to something negative, but that's where my mind went. Nate. Jealousy flooded through me. She was going back to him. Going back to her old life.

Panic and anger made it difficult for me to think straight. If Bree went back to Nate, I wasn't sure what I would do. Could I stay in California? Could I live in the same city with her and Nate together? Then I thought about my mom. Maybe it was a sign. Maybe I was supposed to stay in Dallas with my mother.

"I saw your mom take something," she said.

"What?" I asked shaking my head. "What are you talking about?"

"When I was in the room with her earlier, she grabbed her purse and took some pills. I heard the bottle, but I don't know what it was or how many she took."

"How do you know?" I snapped. "Why would she do that?"

"She doesn't know I can see, remember?" she explained. "I thought maybe it could be mints or something like that, but then not long after she took whatever it was, she had that episode. Do you think it could be related?"

"You know she took something?" I asked.

"Luke, I can't tell you details, but I definitely saw her reach for a bag by her bed. I heard what sounded like pills in a bottle. She put her hand to her mouth and that was that. It was maybe fifteen minutes later that whatever happened, happened."

I slapped my hand against the table, bouncing the plastic trays. "Are you fucking kidding me?" I hissed.

"Luke, I'm sorry. Maybe I'm wrong."

"I need to get back up there. I'll call you a cab and get you back to the hotel."

"Don't be mad at me?" she said. "I'm only telling you what I saw."

"You didn't see anything, remember? You think you saw something. You have no proof."

Her mouth dropped open. "Well, I'm not making it up. What purpose would that serve?"

"I need to get back upstairs," I growled. I was going to search the fucking bag myself.

I got up and waited for her to stand. She did. When I reached for her hand, she yanked it away.

"I'm not lying, Luke."

I ignored her. I was so pissed. I started moving through the cafeteria, frequently checking back to make sure she was behind me. She put on her sunglasses as we moved into the hallway. I stepped outside, the heat of the day a stark contrast to the cool air inside the hospital.

"Bree, I will call you later," I said, as I hailed a cab.

"This is ridiculous. Why would I make something like that up?"

"I'm not saying you did," I said, opening the back door of the cab that pulled to a stop.

"You are acting like I did something wrong."

"Bree, just get in the cab!"

Her mouth dropped open before her lips pursed together. She got in the cab and yanked the door closed. I watched the cab pull away before heading back inside. I knew she was upset, but I couldn't deal with it all at once. I had to find out what the hell my mother was doing. I stomped down the hall, slapping my hand against the elevator button.

It didn't come fast enough. I moved to the stairwell and started climbing. None of it made sense. Why would my mother take pills in front of Bree? I knew Bree's vision was getting better, but was it really good enough to see what she thought she saw? I didn't know what to think. I didn't want to believe my mother could do something so stupid, but then there was that little part of me that had suspected something like that from the beginning.

Chapter Twenty-One

Bree

LAST NIGHT HAD BEEN miserable. Absolutely fucking miserable. I stood in front of the window, the curtains opened just a few inches. It was enough sunlight for me to see Luke lying in bed. One leg hung out from under the sheet, an arm was crooked over his face, like he was shielding himself from something.

We had barely talked at all last night when he returned from the hospital. I didn't want to upset him with my accusations or assumptions. I know what I saw. I know she took something, but I would keep it to myself. Clearly, he didn't want to hear it.

I walked into the bathroom and took a shower. I wasn't sure I was doing much good here in Dallas. I didn't want to be an added stressor to Luke's already full plate. He didn't really need me to worry about on top of his mother's illness. I was going to go home. It was the best thing for us.

When I got out of the bathroom, Luke was waiting with fresh coffee.

"Hi," he said, holding out a cup.

I could see lots of skin. He was wearing nothing but his briefs. He was a sexy man.

"Hi," I said, taking the coffee.

144

"I'm so sorry," he said. "I totally freaked out on you and that was wrong."

I decided this was as good a time as any to clear the air between us. Something was obviously going on and I wasn't interested in being shut out. "Do you want to tell me what is really going on?"

With a groan, he said, "Not really."

It was like a slap to the face. "Okay. Alright. Well, in this case, I think I should just go home."

"Why?"

"Because you have this stuff going on and you don't want me to know about it. I'm in the way. I came to be supportive and I'm not doing that."

"Wait. Just wait."

I could hear the pain in his voice. "Luke, will you just talk to me. Tell me what I can't see, and I mean that in a very literal sense. I know there is something more happening here, and I just don't know what it is. Please. I came here to be with you. You've done so much for me. I want to help you. To support you. And I can't do that if you shut me out. You are keeping something from me. I get it if you want to do that, but I'm not doing you any good sitting here. I'll just go home. Then if and when you are ready to talk, I'll be there."

He grabbed my hand. "Don't leave."

"Luke, you have so much going on, I don't want to make it worse."

"You are not making it worse. Not at all."

I sighed. I didn't want to leave him. "Will you please explain to me what is going on then?"

"Let's sit. I'll order some breakfast."

Sitting down at the small table in the room, I waited. I listened to him order room service before coming to sit at the table.

"Are you okay?"

"I am. I'm just kind of in my head."

"Because of your mom?" I asked.

"Yes. I have long suspected she was making herself sick," he said. "She got seriously ill very fast. It was not that long ago that she managed to travel to California on her own. Suddenly being on dialysis never made sense to me. It doesn't make sense to her doctors, either. I didn't want to think she was doing it on purpose, but now I think I have to face the truth."

"You think the actual illness she is suffering from she caused herself?"

"Yes," he answered.

"Has she done this before?"

He blew out a breath. "I don't know, but I've been going back through time and little things are jumping out."

"Like?"

"Like the time I was supposed to go away for a weekend with a girl I had been seeing for a couple of months. My mom didn't like her, but my mom doesn't like anyone. The girl and I weren't really serious, but I did like her. I was at the library, studying for finals. I was supposed to be leaving that evening to go out of town. I got a call from a paramedic. My mother had fallen while on her way to the grocery store near her house. She broke her wrist and her ankle. Obviously, I had to cancel my plans and stay home to care for her."

I slowly nodded. "And that stands out in your mind because?"

"Because the fall seemed a little extreme, and the timing was off. I had already done the grocery shopping for her. There was no reason for her to go to the store in the first place."

"I see."

He wasn't finished. "Another time, I was at a party with some guys from school. I had been busy all week doing my clinical hours and hadn't had time to visit her. Once again, I got a call. This time, it was from a neighbor who said they heard my mother calling for help. They went into the house and found her lying on the floor, suffering from what she claimed was a heart attack. Again, I rushed to her side and skipped class to take care of her. I nearly failed."

"And you think she faked it?"

"No. It was real, but there was no reason for it. She was in her forties and had no prior heart problems."

I winced, shaking my head. "I'm so sorry."

"Tell me what you think. Be brutally honest. If you were reading this story or watching it on television, what would you think? Don't hold back. Don't try to spare my feelings. I need an outside opinion."

Though I knew what he was asking for, I wasn't sure he really knew what he was asking for. I didn't want him to hate me or get pissed at me for my opinion. "Luke, I don't want to butt my nose in."

"I want you to butt in. Please, Bree. You see people differently."

"I think your mother loves you," I said. "She loves you and doesn't want to lose you."

He waved a hand. "Yeah, yeah, yeah—but?"

Squeezing my eyes shut, I said, "But I think it's an unhealthy relationship."

"Do you think her accidents and illnesses are fake?"

"I don't know. I couldn't possibly know that. I do think there is something suspect about the timing. And, I know you think I'm crazy, but I know what I saw."

"I searched her bag," he said.

"And?"

"I didn't find any pills."

"Okay." I wasn't going to argue with him, but I knew what I had seen. I couldn't know for sure what they were or if it really was mints or something, but I had not smelled mint. My senses were still heightened. I would have picked up on something like menthol or peppermint.

"But I believe you," he said, startling me.

"You do?"

"I do. She was absolutely fine when I walked out of that room. There was no medical reason for her blood pressure to tank like that. The vomiting indicates her body was trying to get rid of something."

"Did you tell her doctor?"

"No."

"Did you ask her about the pills?"

I heard his exhale. "No, not directly. I asked about the moments before the onset, but she claims it just hit."

"You've been dealing with this your whole life?" I asked.

"Yes, basically. It didn't get really bad until the last ten years or so. About the time I turned eighteen and started trying to break away. The more I struggled against the restraints she forced on me, the sicker she got. She got better at making me feel like shit. It got to the point where I felt like I was going to lose my mind. I packed my shit, quit my job and fled to California."

With just a few words, I suddenly had a whole new understanding about who he was. My heart went out to him. I had known about her history, but now, seeing it first-hand, I had a very different picture. "I get it. You've got a lot going on. Is she going to get better?"

"Yes, assuming she stops taking whatever it is she is taking. The dialysis is working. The doctor was ready to drop it down to twice a week and eventually off. There is nothing physically wrong with her. Well, I mean, there is, but it's fixable."

"Is there anything you can do to make her better? Like you personally, only you?"

He hesitated before answering. "Her doctor thinks she would probably get better if she could go home."

"But she would require care?"

"Yes."

"Professional care, from a nurse?"

He sighed again. "Yes. They've asked me to be her caregiver. My mom has asked me to do it."

"Oh, Luke," I said, feeling horrible for him. "What are you going to do?"

"I don't know."

"Can you hire someone?" I asked.

He laughed. "I've tried that before. They either quit or she fires them."

"Because she wants you."

"Yes. Only I know how to do it."

"I see," I said, mulling over the predicament. "I think you are an excellent nurse, and please don't take this the wrong way, but I don't think you are the only person in this big city that can do what you do."

He laughed. "I think you are very right."

"If she's sick enough to need someone, then I think she's going to have to decide between someone you hire or staying in the hospital."

"Can you give me a couple hours?" he asked.

"What do you mean?"

"I want to go over to the hospital and check on things. I know some nurses that need to pick up side work. I want to see if anyone is willing to act as her nurse."

I nodded, understanding what he was doing. He was tidying up the mess so he could leave. "Go see your mom. I'll be here waiting."

"Breakfast should be here any minute," he said. "I'm going to hop in the shower."

"Go, I'll take care of it."

I sat in the chair, mulling over what he had told me. I couldn't imagine the emotional abuse Luke had suffered. It was abuse. His mother was trying to control him. She was crazy. She was cruel. Part of me wanted to shake her and ask her how she could treat her son like that. Luke bent over backwards to make her happy and she shit all over him.

The woman didn't realize what she was doing to him. If she did realize it, she was even crueler than I thought. The man was suffering. He was being eaten alive by guilt he had no reason to feel. She was hurting him just for the sake of hurting him.

Room service arrived about a minute before he got out of the shower. "Aren't you going to eat first?" I asked, when I heard him pick up the keys.

"No. I'm good."

"Take some toast," I told him.

He gave me a quick kiss, grabbed a slice of toast and rushed out the door. I prayed it went well. I hoped there was some miracle recovery overnight and all would be well. I wanted Luke to be freed from the burden that was his mother.

It would be great if they could have an actual relationship, a healthy relationship. Watching and hearing about Luke and his mom made me appreciate my father that much more. I wanted to do everything I could to make his life a little easier. Now that my sight was better, I didn't have to rely on him so much. The man needed some time to breathe. He needed some time to find himself without having to take care of someone.

We could be together like a normal couple, not a nursemaid and invalid. I finished eating and started to pack. I was going to get him out of Dallas. Once I got him back to California, I would dote on him. We would go to the beach and just relax. We would get to know each other better as a couple.

We wouldn't talk about my eyesight or his mother's illness.

Chapter Twenty-Two

Luke

I WALKED OUT OF HER hospital room feeling defeated. She had suffered another episode. I didn't know how to help her. She was doing it to herself. I knew it for certain. She needed help from a mental health professional. I had tried to talk to her over and over and it always ended in tears and denial.

Rubbing a hand over my face, I didn't know what to do. She was ill. That was a fact. If I could get her home, get her well again, then maybe I could convince her to seek counseling. Maybe then we could have a normal relationship. I hoped it would happen. Then again, I had been hoping it would happen for so long and it never did.

I drove back to the hotel, looking forward to seeing Bree. She was my calm in the storm. She was my life raft. She understood. It was strange to have her know my story—all of it. She knew and she didn't think I was a freak. Lisa, my own sister, thought I was a freak. She acted like I was damaged. Like I was somehow encouraging my mother to be crazy.

I finally had an ally. I walked down the hallway, feeling much lighter than I had when I had been at the hospital. I slid my keycard in the lock, hoping to surprise her.

"Hello?" I called out.

"Hey," she said, getting up from the chair on the balcony. "I wasn't expecting you back so soon."

I walked in and froze when I spotted the suitcases sitting on the bed.

"What's that?" I asked pointing to the bed, before remembering she probably couldn't see me pointing. "On the bed."

"Suitcases."

"Why are they on the bed?"

"Because I didn't want to leave them on the floor."

She was being coy.

"Bree," I said her name.

"I booked our flights home. We leave tonight."

My brows shot up. "You did what?"

"I booked our flights. I figured I would take it off your plate."

"Why did you book our flights? For tonight?"

She stepped closer to me, tilting her head to the side. "Because we are going home. I thought you were setting up homecare for your mom, so we could go home."

I shook my head. "I didn't say that."

"You said you were going to see if someone needed extra shifts."

"I'm sorry you misunderstood, but I've thought about it and I'm staying."

It was her turn to look shocked. "For how long?"

I shrugged. "I don't know. I was thinking we could stay here for a week, maybe two. I'll stick around until she is well enough to be on her own and then go back to California."

"But my gallery," she said.

"Your gallery with Nate," I snapped.

"With Nate? It isn't with Nate. Anton is a mutual friend. Nate isn't involved, and so what if he was? You really have to get over this jealousy thing."

"Jealousy thing? Look who's jealous."

She threw up her hands. "What are you talking about? Are you suggesting I'm jealous of your mother?"

"Why are you trying to drag me away after two days?"

"Because we sat here this morning talking about her manipulating you to be here."

I shook my head. "She might be, but that doesn't change the fact she is sick. She needs care. Her insurance is going to kick her out of the hospital soon. Unlike some people, I can't afford to put her in some fancy home. I'm it. I'm the guy that has to make sure she doesn't die."

"You are not the only guy that can do that," she shot back.

"I knew I shouldn't have told you about her. You are using it as an excuse to get away. I guess I don't blame you. You are fleeing the freaks."

"I am not!" she protested. "I am doing what you said you wanted to do."

"I never said I was going to go anywhere."

"You said you knew she was messing with you. This is her trying to keep you here. I told you she took pills to make herself sick and you believed me. Now, you don't? Did she give you some story about it being mints? Because I thought about it, and it wasn't. I would have smelled the mint."

"It's cool. I don't expect you to stick around. This is not your problem. You've got a gallery to open."

"That's not fair!"

I smirked. "It's not like you can't open the gallery in a week or two. I mean, what are you going to do, throw up a sign and announce you are open for business. Don't you have to actually have art?"

She was quiet for a few seconds. "No, I don't have art but there are meetings that need to happen. What exactly do you think you are going to do here? She is sucking you right back into the situation you just escaped from. You have to know what is happening. You have to see what she is doing."

"You don't even know what you are talking about," I snapped.

"I think I do. Lisa tried to warn you to stay away from this place. I get it now. She loves and is looking out for you. I love you and I don't want to see you hurt by these games. She's toying with you. When do you plan on living your life?"

"I have to help her," I insisted. "I can't just leave her here, all alone."

She closed her eyes and took a deep breath. "Luke, you need to decide what you want. Me and our life in California, or giving your every waking moment to her here in Dallas."

"I should have known. I knew you wouldn't get it."

"I do get it. I understand you are being pulled in two different directions. I feel terrible about that, but I think you are doing yourself a huge disservice if you choose to stay here."

"That's your opinion."

"I offered to come here and support you because I wanted to. I still want to, but I also have my own dreams I want to chase."

"The gallery," I said.

"Yes. You know I've wanted this. You brought me here to show me the art. I thought you were on board with it."

Since we were being so open and honest, I decided to drop the little bombshell I had been holding. "You don't find it the least bit coincidental that this guy has just shown up in your life?"

She looked confused. "What guy?"

"The gallery guy! Nate's friend!"

"He didn't just show up. He spoke with Nate and heard about my accident and that I was healing. Anton and I used to talk about opening a gallery before he moved away. Now that he's back, he wants to do it. It isn't that crazy."

"The timing seems a little too convenient for me," I told her.

"Would it be better if it was inconvenient?"

"Your father and Nate are working together to get the two of you back together," I blurted out.

"Oh my goodness. That is about the most ridiculous thing I've ever heard."

"It isn't ridiculous. I heard them."

She sighed, shaking her head. "You heard them what? Plotting?"

"Actually, yes."

"What're you talking about?"

She was looking at me like I was crazy and I realized I sounded like a lunatic and nothing but the truth would do. "I was on my way over to the house and happened to come upon the two of them talking."

"And they were plotting to help me open a gallery? The horrors! We should hang them out to dry."

"No. Your father wants you back together with Nate. Why do you think he hired him? Nate is trying to win you back. I'm guessing your dad will be footing the bill for this gallery."

She held up a hand. "You're going too far."

"Bree, listen to me. Your father wants you with Nate and he is working to make that happen. He and Nate probably reached out to this Anton guy."

"Anton and I are going to discuss a joint partnership."

"And he has the money for half? You don't think that maybe your father is putting up that half? I bet it's going to be something like he's a silent partner and you get the business all to yourself. Your dad gets what he wants, and Nate gets you back."

She rolled her eyes. "I'm going home. You can figure out what you want, but I'm not going to sit here and watched you get jerked around. You are her puppet. She's pulling all the strings. I hate to see you treated that way but if you won't help yourself, there is little I can do for you."

"I'm not a fucking puppet."

"I'll catch a cab to the airport."

I couldn't believe she was just going to walk out on me. I watched her move around the room, collecting her things. She was pissed. I couldn't remember her ever being pissed. She stuffed some things in her purse and grabbed her suitcase from the bed. She stood staring at me. She was waiting for me to stop her. I wasn't going to. If she wanted to walk out on me, that was her choice.

"Tell Nate I said hi," I muttered.

"Wow," she whispered. "You're different when your mother is around."

I said nothing, but walked to the door and opened it. I was pissed that she was leaving me, but I wasn't going to let her walk out of the hotel on her own.

"What are you doing?" she asked, when I followed her into the elevator.

"I'm walking you out."

"I don't need your help. I can see well enough."

"Bree, I don't want you in the airport alone," I said, suddenly terrified at the idea.

"You are welcome to come with me," she said.

"I can't."

"You can. You choose not to. There's a big difference."

I said nothing more. I got her into the cab and watched her go. My heart hurt watching her leave. Part of me wanted to chase after her. A big part of me. Obligation kept me from doing that. I couldn't just up and leave my mother.

I wouldn't be surprised to learn I had nothing to go back to. I had really blown it with Bree. I sounded like a jealous boyfriend lashing out in an attempt to save my relationship. Instead of saving it, I was pretty sure I had just destroyed it. I had just pushed her right into Nate's waiting arms. I wouldn't be the least bit surprised to find out I was fired, and my things were being shipped back to Dallas tomorrow.

Once Paul found out what I had done, he would be furious. He would kick me out and I really couldn't blame him for doing it. Even now, I was fighting the need to chase after her. She seemed to get around the room fairly well and I had to trust her to do it on her own.

Heading back up to the room, I was miserable. It felt big and empty without her stuff scattered about. I took my suitcase off the bed and dropped it on the floor before flopping onto the bed. I was making a mess of my life. A huge fucking mess. It was like I was staring at the map, staring at the road signs directing me to the right path and I kept choosing the wrong way. I was an idiot.

Chapter Twenty-Three

Bree

I'D ARRIVED FAR TOO early for my flight. I had shown up at the airport and realized it had been foolish to think I could get through the crazy crowds with my shitty vision. I had been bumped and bounced around to the point that I felt like a ping pong ball. I had to keep the sunglasses off to see anything. I needed every advantage. I could feel the headache coming on from straining to see. Pushing through the panic, I made my way to the terminal to wait it out.

Finding a seat out of the way, I hugged my purse close. I closed my eyes, praying I could see better when I opened them again. Opening my eyes, I scanned the area. Now that I was out of the crowd, I could relax. A flight attendant would see me to my seat, which just happened to be in first class. It was supposed to be a surprise for Luke.

Part of me kept thinking Luke would show up. Deep down, I could admit that I wanted him to chase me. I wanted him to choose me and our life together in California. I had truly believed he wanted to leave Texas. I wasn't sure what had happened at the hospital, but whatever it was had pulled Luke right back into her web of lies and deceit. She was probably doing a victory lap in her room, celebrating her win. How any mother could claim to love a child and then treat him like that as beyond me. She didn't love him. She loved herself. She was willing to destroy his life for her own need for attention.

I pushed the thoughts aside. I wasn't going to try and figure out something that no one else had been able to, including her own son. I had a lot of time to kill, so I pulled out my phone and called Mel. I couldn't wait to tell her about the gallery. Luke may not be happy, but I knew Mel would be.

"Hey there," she answered. "Are you wearing cowboy boots?"

"No. Actually, I'm sitting in the airport."

"You guys are coming back already?"

"Not exactly," I said, realizing I had a lot to tell her and a couple hours with nothing to do but chat. I grabbed my purse and moved to another seat out of the way with no one else around. "I'm coming home alone."

"Oh, Bree, is that safe?"

"Are you talking about my eyes or the plane crashing?"

"Your eyes," she said. "Is his mom really sick?"

"No. Yes, but not because she's sick. I mean, she's sick, but she's sick on purpose."

Mel was quiet for a second. "What in the hell are you saying? Are you drunk? What time is it there?"

"I'm not drunk. His mom is like a hypochondriac on steroids. She didn't know I could see. When Luke left the room, she took some pills and suddenly she was on death's door with everyone fawning all over her."

"You sound a little bitter," she lectured.

"No. I'm not. She is messing with Luke's head. It's sad. It's screwing with him and it pisses me off. She hates me. She thinks I took her precious son away. This little tactic is just the latest in a long line of stunts she has pulled. She likes to be sick so he will dote on her."

"Weird. Really weird."

"It is."

"So, he's staying? Like for good?"

I sighed. "I honestly don't know. We had a fight and I left."

"And he let you?" she shrieked. "I'm going to kick his ass myself!"

"It's fine. I can see a lot better than I did even a few days ago."

"Really? That's awesome, but still. That is no excuse. You went there to be with him. He shouldn't be letting you hang out at the airport by yourself."

"I'm a big girl," I reminded her.

"I'm sorry," she said. "I really liked him."

"I really like him still. I'm giving him a day or two. If he doesn't figure it out, then I guess I'll know he plans on staying in Dallas."

"I know he loves you. I have a feeling he will show up at the airport and you guys will have one of those dramatic reunions with a big kiss. He'll swoop you up into his arms and swing you around. I wish I was there to see it."

I laughed. "I think that would be lovely but I'm not going to hold my breath. But that's not why I called, actually."

"You need me to pick you up from the airport?"

At that moment, I realized I actually did need her to pick me up. "Yes, actually, that would be great, but no, not that."

"Okay." She was silent for a few seconds. "Am I supposed to guess? If so, you need to give me a hint."

I laughed. "Sorry, I was spacing out. I'm opening a gallery!"

"I know that. You knew that before you left."

"No, I talked about starting the process, but now I'm skipping ahead and doing it."

"You found a space?"

I quickly told her about Anton and the offer to form a partnership. "Do you think it's weird that he called me out of the blue?" I asked.

"I don't know. I know who he is, but I didn't know him all that well. Why? Do you think something is up?"

"Luke told me he thinks my dad and Nate are trying to get me back with Nate."

She laughed. "Well, that isn't so far-fetched."

"Really?"

"Bree, come on. You know your father. And you know he likes to get what he wants. He liked Nate."

"But Luke thinks my dad and Nate are actually scheming. He thinks my dad and Nate conspired with Anton to open the gallery. He thinks my dad is putting up the investment money for Anton. Would he do that?"

She was quiet. "I don't know. I wish I could say no, but honestly, I don't know. Your dad is a powerful man. I love him like my own dad, but he can be pushy. He can throw his weight around and by that, I mean he throws around his money."

"Nate and my dad have always been against me opening a gallery. Why would they suddenly work together to make it a thing?"

"I don't know. Maybe they want to make you happy. Nate might think if you are happy, it will be easier for him to work his way in. Since he and Anton are friends, it's a good way for him to see you more. There could be events for couples and eventually you and he would be a couple again."

It did make sense and it was something Nate would do, but I didn't think my dad would be involved. "That isn't going to happen. I broke up with him for a reason."

"Before you buy into too much of the conspiracy theory stuff, I would talk with Anton. This could all be a very innocent proposal."

"I'm going to call Anton tomorrow and set up a meeting. I'll know more then."

"Are you going to ask your dad?"

I groaned. "Do I have to?"

"No, but then you're always going to wonder."

"That should be a fun conversation," I mumbled.

"I'll see you tonight," she said.

"Thanks."

I stayed put, out of the way of the hustle and bustle. I was starving, but I didn't dare try to make my way around the food court. I would eat when I got back to Malibu. I spent the next two hours making notes on my tablet about what I wanted to talk to Anton about. I had a lot of questions. I wasn't interested in taking any charity. If I found out my dad had meddled in the deal, I would walk away.

Could I walk away? I wanted the gallery. As much as I wanted to open a gallery, I could admit I needed some help. Anton had the experience and I could learn from him. I didn't want to open a gallery and fail right out of the gate. Even if my father's money was involved, I was still leaning towards accepting the help.

Hearing my flight called, I slowly made my way to the gate. I talked with a very sweet flight attendant who led me to my seat. I settled in, putting on my sunglasses and closing my eyes. I was exhausted after trying to see everything in the airport, so I needed to rest my eyes to prepare for my next airport experience.

By the time I heard Mel calling my name, I was more than ready to be home in the safety and comfort of my own bedroom. She grabbed hold of me and immediately I felt relief wash over me.

"Can you please help me get my suitcase. I didn't think about that when I checked it."

She laughed. "I suppose, but you better tip me well."

"I'll buy you a hamburger. I'm starving."

"And fries," she ordered.

I laughed. "And a shake."

Twenty minutes later, we were sitting in her car and scarfing down junk food. She drove me home after we had successfully put away more food than two proper young women should ever eat. I waved goodbye and headed inside. It was after eleven and I was exhausted.

I walked into my bedroom, dropped my suitcase and headed for my bed. It felt strange to be home without Luke nearby. I wondered what he was doing before remembering the time difference. He was likely sleeping.

But I didn't want to be without him. I hated the idea of not being able to talk to him or see his face for the first time. To really see his face. I had been so close. I wasn't sure if he would ever come back to California. He seemed pretty set on staying in Texas. His mom was likely going to drag out the sick thing for weeks. She would never willingly let Luke go. If he couldn't find the strength to walk away, he would never be free of her and stuck in limbo forever.

I felt horrible for him. It was awful that he was stuck in that life. I understood his reasons for wanting to stay and I understood the hold she had over him. It didn't make it any easier to accept. I wanted him to be free. I wanted him to be able to live a life he enjoyed.

Thinking about spending the next days, weeks and even longer without him hurt. I could feel the sadness hovering and refused to give in. After witnessing what Charlene had done, I realized how much of my own troubles were mind over matter. I didn't have to let the sadness win. I could be strong. The last thing Luke needed was another woman dragging him down.

If he came back, and if he wanted to have a relationship with me after what had been said, I would promise to be a stronger person. I sighed, rolling over to my side and kicking off my shoes. Tomorrow, I would confront my father.

Chapter Twenty-Four

Luke

I FELT LIKE AN EMPTY shell. Hollow inside. Bree's absence had shaken me to my core. I had never felt so empty inside and didn't realize just how important she had become in my life until she was gone. That saying about not knowing what you had until it was gone was very real in this case. My heart felt broken.

And I knew what I wanted. I knew what the right choice was. My misery was truly of my own making. After going back to the hospital to spend some time with my mother, I had come back to the empty hotel room. I'd kept hoping I would find her there when I returned. Hoping a change of heart would have brought her back.

I held my phone in my hand, staring at the picture of us together. We had taken it yesterday in front of a statue. I smiled, staring at her beautiful face and her smile that had been so bright. She had been happy, truly happy. I had no business trying to destroy that. Bree, of all the people I knew, deserved to be happy. She had lived through hell and had every right to be that happy.

Over and over, I thought about texting. I thought about calling. But did neither. I was a coward, and I felt like a complete asshole for what I had done. Now I didn't know what to say to her. I'm sorry felt wholly inadequate. I owed her a lot more than sorry.

Closing my eyes, I tried to sleep. Housekeeping had put on fresh sheets, stealing away her scent. I hugged the extra pillow close. We only had a couple nights together in the same bed, but I felt her absence deeply. I slept better with her body against mine. I slept better with the scent of her filling my every inhaled breath.

When I woke early the next morning, I knew what I had to do. It was what I should have done yesterday. I showered and dressed before heading to the hospital. I smiled and nodded to the nurses that were just coming on for the coveted dayshift. In the ED, everyone wanted the dayshift. It was supposed to be easier. I liked the excitement of the noc shift myself. I liked the craziness, and I missed it.

Walking into my mother's room, I was thankful to see that she was still asleep. It was the reason I showed up so early. My mother loved her beauty sleep. I opened the little closet where patient's personal belongings were stored and rummaged through the bag. When I didn't find what I was looking for, I looked around her bed and then by the chair next to the window.

I saw her purse sitting in the corner, a discarded hand towel over it. To the average person, it would look innocent enough. I saw a cover up. She was trying to conceal the purse that was within reach of the chair she was put in during the day. I had searched the purse yesterday, but not well.

Snatching it up and with my back to my mother, I unzipped it and rummaged around. I shook the purse and heard the sound of pills but didn't see the bottle. I stuck my hand inside and felt around. Nothing. Finally, using two hands to squeeze the different sections, I felt the bottle and realized it was inside a zippered pouch in the middle. I unzipped it, pissed that I hadn't noticed the damn thing the day before. I pulled out a bottle of Tylenol.

Popping open the lid, I dumped a few pills into my palm. It wasn't fucking Tylenol. I carried the pills into the hall and did a quick Google search on my phone to find out what they were. They were blood pressure meds, which wouldn't be a big deal, but too many and it could cause kidney failure. It explained everything.

"Fuck me," I whispered, shaking my head and going back into the room.

"Luke, is that you?" my mother mumbled, still half asleep.

"Yes, it's me. Wake up, Mom. We need to talk."

She made a big show about sitting up in the bed. "What's wrong?"

I held up the bottle and shook it. "This is what's wrong. You did this to yourself. You've been taking pills that aren't prescribed to you to make yourself sick. Do you know what these do to your body?"

"How dare you—"

"Save it. Bree saw you and I just found the pills in your purse. Do you want to die?"

"How can you say that to me?" she gasped. "Look at me. I'm hooked to machines on hovering at death's door."

"Only because you want to be. You did this to yourself. What the hell were you thinking? Do you realize you could have died? You could have given yourself a stroke or gone into a coma. What other shit have you been taking? Do the doctors know you have this stuff?"

She was caught and she knew it. "I wasn't feeling good and the doctor couldn't get me in. A friend hooked me up with some old medicine."

I shook my head. "Bullshit. You did this on purpose. You know more about pharmaceuticals than any doctor I have ever met. You knew exactly what you were doing."

"No," she protested.

"I can't believe you did this. I can't believe you purposely tried to kill yourself."

"I did no such thing! I wasn't feeling well and took some medicine. I didn't know it would make me sick."

I scoffed. "Yes, you did. You've been taking this because you wanted me to come back. You knew what would happen if you took too many.

You made yourself sick and I came running. That's exactly what you wanted. The emotional blackmail is old and I can't do it anymore. I won't do it anymore."

She shook her head, tears streaming down her face. "No. You don't understand. I've been so lonely."

I looked at her, really looked at her. She was a sick woman. "I'm going to get coffee," I said, and walked out of the room before things got really ugly.

She called out after me, but I kept going. I couldn't explain how I felt. Everything felt wrong. It was like waking up from a nightmare only to find out it wasn't a nightmare at all. It was me waking up and discovering the bulk of my life had been spent being manipulated.

My intention was to go to the little coffee shop next to the cafeteria. Instead, I found myself outside calling my sister.

"What's up?" she answered. "Is it real?"

I groaned, walking to a bench under a tall tree and sitting down. "No. Yes, it's real, but she did it."

"What did she do?"

"She made herself sick. Like really sick. Bree saw her taking pills. I just searched her purse and found them."

She sighed. "What were they?"

"Blood pressure meds. She doesn't have high blood pressure. It damaged her kidneys and caused her vitals to bottom out yesterday."

"Is she going to live?" she asked, in a somber tone.

"If she quits taking these stupid pills, yes."

"I know you aren't actually surprised by this. You and I have both long suspected this was what she was doing. What does Bree say?"

I looked down at my scuffed tennis shoes. "She said a lot and then she left. She asked me to choose between staying here and essentially being mom's bitch, or going back with her."

"I guess I don't have to ask what you chose. Give me a second to scream at your stupidity and then I will be right back with you."

"Thanks for the support," I said dryly.

"I told you, don't go. I told you, it was bullshit. I hate to say I told you so, but Luke, I told you."

"You certainly don't act like you are hating to say it."

"I'm sorry. No, I'm not sorry. Dammit Luke. You are one of the smartest people I know, and I don't understand how you cannot get out from under her thumb. She's using you. She's abusing you. She's slowly killing you. You will never find happiness if you don't tell that woman to knock her shit off. You are probably the only person she will ever listen to."

"I screwed up," I said, feeling the weight of the world on my shoulders. "I really screwed up."

"Bree is a pretty awesome chick. I think if you pull your head out of your ass and properly grovel, you have a good chance at winning her back. But the only way you can do that is if you tell your mother to get her shit together."

"She's your mom too," I argued.

"That's debatable. I don't remember coming out of her body and unless someone can give me video proof, I'm going to dispute any such allegation."

I had to laugh at the absurdity of it all. "What am I supposed to do now? Everyone here thinks I need to take her home and nurse her back to health."

"Everyone there doesn't know what she is like. She needs to be in a mental hospital and I'm not even saying that to be mean. She has issues and she is forcing those issues on you. Cut the cord. It's time. It's way past time."

I could always count on Lisa to be blunt. I was pretty sure living in the UK the last decade had made her even more tactless. She had no filter. "And what if she dies? I don't think I can live with myself if she does."

"If she dies, you have to treat it as a suicide. It will be by her own hand. You've tried. You have sacrificed everything to be there for her. She needs help."

"Thanks. I'm going to go back in and try to talk to her. I doubt it will work."

"If it doesn't, you get your ass on that plane and you go back to Malibu. You go back to Bree and you plead temporary insanity. Tell her you have come to your senses and you will never be so stupid again."

I laughed. "You really know how to make a guy feel good about himself."

"Be strong. I'm behind you all the way."

"Thanks."

I ended the call and while I was still riding high on her rather abrupt pep talk, I headed back to my mother's room. She was sitting up in bed, drinking from her fresh cup of ice water.

"Are you over your little temper tantrum?" she asked.

Slowly, I shook my head. "It's not a tantrum. This is it for me. Truly. I cannot and will not do this anymore. You have the means to be healthy. If you choose not to do that, it's on you. I will not be your little nursemaid anymore."

"I don't know what you think you found, but your little girlfriend is a liar."

"No, she isn't. You are. If you want me to be a part of your life, you need to seek therapy."

"For what?" she snapped.

"For whatever issues you have that are causing you to make yourself sick. You need help. Mental help. I cannot do this anymore. This is an illness that goes beyond all these machines and the medicines. This is something you need to work on with a therapist."

She frowned. "Are you saying I'm nuts?"

I shrugged. "If that's what you want to call it. You need help. You are not well and I'm not talking in a physical sense. I can arrange to have you taken to another facility to get the attention you need, but I won't be here."

"What are you saying?" she whimpered.

"I'm saying, that unless you seek treatment for the disease that is causing you to make yourself sick, I cannot be a part of your life."

"What! How can you say that! I'm your mother."

"Yes, you are and it's why I have stuck it out for as long as I have, but I won't do it anymore. I value my life and I want to be happy. You are set on making me miserable. I'm not going to let you do that anymore. I am taking back my own power."

"You're so dramatic. You sound just like your sister."

"I wish I was more like her. I would have done this a long time ago. Now, I have to go. I've got a flight to catch. I need to try and repair the damage I've done to the best thing to ever happen to me. I do hope you will make the right decision. If you want to check into a facility, I will make a call. If you choose not to, I will not be back. You are going to push your body too far one of these days and do more damage than can be repaired. It's up to you what happens next."

I walked out before she had a chance to dump another guilt trip on me. I didn't have a flight, but I was going to get on the next one out of Dallas.

Chapter Twenty-Five

Bree

I WALKED INTO THE DINING room, prepared to confront my father about the Nate situation. I was not going to let him see the fear and anger. The more I thought about what Luke said, the more inclined I was to believe it was true.

"Good morning," I said, walking in, quite impressed with my vision. I could make out the coffee cup and dishes on the table.

"Good morning sweetheart. I didn't know you were coming in last night."

"It was kind of an unplanned return."

"Did Luke make the trip back with you?"

"No."

He reached for his cup of coffee and took a drink. "Will he be staying in Dallas?"

"Would you like him to stay in Dallas?"

"What does that mean?"

"It means, why are you so against me being with him?"

He put the coffee down and turned to me. I had a general idea of his facial features, so it was easy to imagine him looking at me. "Why would you think that?"

I mustered my courage. "Dad, are you trying to get me back with Nate?"

"What? Why would I get involved in all that?"

The way he said it told me he was lying. If I could have clearly seen his eyes, I would be able to tell for certain. "Because you don't like Luke. You don't think he's good enough for me. You've always liked Nate, even though he is not a man I will ever love."

"It's not that I don't like the guy, but I still feel he took advantage of you."

"He didn't. I promise you; he did not do that. He isn't like that. He is an honorable man. You didn't answer my question; are you trying to get me and Nate back together?"

He cleared his throat. "I wouldn't say I was trying, but I do want you to be happy."

His lack of a denial was an admission. "Dad, I'm going to say this one last time. Nate and I are over. It was over for a good year before I finally ended it. He is not the man for me. He doesn't believe in me. He doesn't support me. I don't think he ever will. He's probably going to make some woman very happy, but it won't be me. Please stop trying to push me back with him."

"I suppose you think Luke is the right man for you?"

"I don't know. I do know we have fun together and that he supports me. He understands me and doesn't try to fix me to make me the person he thinks I should be."

I heard my father's sigh of resignation. "I thought you and Nate were happy together. I only want you to be happy."

"Nate doesn't want me for me. He wants a version of me, but it isn't me. I don't think he's a bad guy but Dad, I just don't want to be with him and no matter what lengths you go to, I am not going to be. Can you support me in that?"

"Yes. I will. I'm sorry."

"I have another question, and please be honest."

"What is it?" he asked.

"Did you or Nate, or the two of you together talk to someone about me opening a gallery?"

"What? No. I didn't. I know you said you were thinking about it, but I have certainly not told anyone."

"A man named Anton called me and asked me to be his partner. Anton is an old friend of Nate's. Did Nate ask you to encourage this or ask you to put up the investment?"

"No," he said firmly. "Absolutely not. I don't need to give you any money. You have the inheritance from your mother. If you choose to open a gallery, I will be happy to support you, but that will be on your own dime."

I grinned. That was the dad I was used to. He spoiled me, but also insisted I learn the value of a dollar. I had squandered my allowance too many times to count. When it was gone, it was gone, no matter how much I begged for money for a new purse or shoes.

"Okay. I believe you."

"Alright. Now tell me about this Anton and this gallery."

I smiled and happily filled him in. "I'm meeting him in an hour to talk about it. I'm excited for this, Dad. I really am. This is what I'm supposed to do in this life. I just know it."

He laughed. "I'm happy to see you happy. That's all I have ever wanted for you."

"Thanks, Dad. I'm going to shower and get ready to go."

"Bree," he said, stopping me just before I walked out.

"Yes?"

"Does this mean you can see?"

I laughed. "I can see. It's getting there. I'm still nowhere near twenty-twenty, but I can see well enough to get around."

"Good to know."

I rushed to my room, anxious to meet with Anton and check out the space he had his eye on. I was hoping that by the time the ink was dry on the contracts I would insist we had in place, I would have my full vision back. Ellis had warned me that I might need glasses to correct my vision if it didn't come back quite as good as it had been. I was okay with that.

It was still a little strange to be getting around on my own. I was so used to having a chaperone. I walked into the quaint little café near the beach where Anton was supposed to meet me. It had been a while since I had seen him, but I was hoping I would be able to identify him with my current vision status.

"Bree," I heard my name.

I turned in the direction of the voice and saw a hand waving. I slowly and carefully made my way towards him. "Anton?" I asked.

"It's me, have a seat."

I reached out, found my chair and sat down, breathing a sigh of relief that I had actually made it. "That was interesting."

He chuckled. "I suppose we could have met at your house or somewhere a little more convenient. It's hard to imagine you as not being able to pick up and go."

I smiled. "You and me both, but it's getting there. I'm hoping by this time next week I will be right as rain."

"I have no doubt in my mind that you will."

"Let's talk about this gallery," I said. I was anxious and I wanted to get all the details. Mostly, I wanted to find out if Nate was involved in any way.

We spent the next two hours talking. By the time I walked through the door at home, I was confident that Nate had nothing to do with it. I was thrilled to finally be taking steps toward making my dream come true. It had taken a near death experience to make me realize what I wanted out of life. I wasn't going to waste a single minute.

My dad was gone for a few days, which meant I had the house to myself. Normally, that would make me anxious. Not anymore. I was looking forward to the freedom and independence. I walked to the kitchen to grab a snack when I caught movement out on the patio.

Slowly, I walked towards the door, straining my eyes. I smiled when I recognized the mannerisms of what I had first thought was an intruder. It was Luke. I opened the doors and stepped outside. I didn't need perfect vision to see the massive bouquet of flowers sitting on the patio table.

"You're here!" he exclaimed.

"I was about to say the same thing to you. You're back."

He picked up the flowers and brought them to me. "I am. For you."

I smiled, seeing the general shape and knew they were lilies in a variety of pretty colors. "These are beautiful. Thank you."

"I'm sorry, Bree," he blurted out, putting the flowers back on the table. "I'm so sorry. I was a total dumbass and I am so, so, so sorry for treating you like that. I should never have let you go. I should have begged you to stay or come with you."

"Luke, things were a mess. You had a lot on your plate."

His hands were on my shoulders. "That's true, but that doesn't make what I did right. I want to be with you. You are my priority. I want us to be an official couple. I want to be the man you can count on. I want to be the person you can tell something to and be believed. I should have believed you. What's crazy is that I did believe you, I just didn't want to face it."

"What about your mom?" I asked. "Are you going to be bouncing back and forth? I can't live in Texas. My home is here and frankly, I don't think you should live near her."

"I'm not going back. I searched my mom's purse again and I found the pills. You were right. I should have kept looking until I found them that day."

"So, what happens now with your mom?" I asked. I was thrilled with all that he was saying, but the pull the woman had over him was very strong. If he wasn't willing to walk away from her, it was just going to keep happening. I didn't want to watch him go through that kind of pain and suffering. I couldn't watch him and not say something, which would inevitably lead to another fight.

"She is being transferred to a new facility tomorrow. I reached out to a therapist and she will hopefully get the help she needs. I told her I couldn't be in her life if she continued doing what she was doing and refused to be in therapy to get to the bottom of her real illness."

I could hear the pain in his voice. I stepped forward, offering him a hug. "That must have been really hard."

His arms came around me. "It was, but it was the right thing to do. I wish I would have done it years ago. Can you forgive me?"

"There is nothing to forgive," I assured him. "There is something I need to tell you though."

"What is it?" he asked, holding me close.

"I asked my dad about the Nate situation. While he didn't come right out and confess what was going on, I know you were right. He had this idea I was happy with Nate before. Part of that is my fault. I kept the problems I was having with Nate to myself for a really long time. I hid my unhappiness from him and let him believe everything was okay."

"And Nate?" he asked.

I shrugged. "Nate is Nate. He is not the man I want or need. You are. You have to trust me."

"I do trust you."

"That didn't sound very believable," I said, with a small laugh.

"I trust you with all my heart. It's him I don't trust."

That part I understood. I trusted Luke, but not Charlene. "I guess it's something we are going to have to work on. I want us to be together. I want to be with you."

"Then I will work hard to pretend Nate doesn't exist. I won't turn into a snarling, jealous beast every time he comes sniffing around, but I will let him know you are mine."

I smiled at the declaration. "Am I, huh?"

He gave my ass a good squeeze. "You are."

"My dad is out of town for a couple days," I said, in a low voice.

"My place or yours?" he asked without hesitation.

I laughed. "Just so nobody barges in, lets choose yours."

The next thing I knew, he lifted me up and my legs went around his strong hips. I was going to be very happy with him.

Chapter Twenty-Six

Luke

I TOOK MY LAPTOP OUT to the small table on the patio outside the cottage. I needed to find a job. Bree and I were moving forward with our relationship. She no longer needed a nurse, so I was officially unemployed. I was simply her boyfriend. I loved being her boyfriend. It made me very happy. I had dropped her off at the location they had chosen for the gallery and come back to the cottage to start my job search again.

Bree had all but moved into the cottage with me. I didn't get the impression that the move pleased Paul, but he didn't say much against it. Bree's sight was almost fully back, but for some minor issues with seeing spots now and again. Paul apparently recognized his daughter was back in fighting form and was taking life by the horns once again.

Now, I needed to prove I was worthy of being with her and find myself a damn job. I couldn't believe how difficult it was. Then again, I was being a little picky. I didn't want the graveyard shift. I wanted to spend my nights with Bree. She was going to be working all day while she got the gallery up and running. I didn't want to be working opposite schedules. We would be two ships passing in the night and never see each other.

My phone rang and I quickly answered it, hoping it was a potential job. "Hello?"

"Luke, it's Paul," he said.

"Hi, Paul."

"Are you going to be back at the house anytime soon?"

I looked up towards the main house. "I'm here."

"Oh. Great. I'll be right there."

I stared at the phone in my hand. That was odd. I wasn't expecting him to be home in the middle of a weekday. Sure enough, a minute later he was strolling up the path towards me. I got to my feet and shook his hand. "Nice to see you. Did you get back last night?"

He nodded. "I did. I wanted to talk to you about something."

It didn't sound good. I knew things had been too easy. This was the part where he offered to write me a check if I would go away and leave his daughter alone. I thought about what I would say, how I would reject his offer. "What's up?" I asked.

"I have a friend, an acquaintance really, he's been working with a group for quite some time. He finally got the funding needed to open a clinic here in Malibu."

I nodded, not entirely sure why he was telling me. "Congratulations."

"He needs staff, specifically a nurse. The clinic will cater to the lower income folks that tend to kind of be forgotten in this area. He needs someone with experience dealing with a variety of issues, beyond the basic cough and fever. Your resume stated you worked in a busy emergency room, correct?"

I nodded. "I did for a couple years."

"I gave him your name and passed along the resume you sent me. I've given you a good recommendation. Is this something you would be interested in?"

I was shocked. Floored actually. Speechless even. I bobbed my head up and down. "Yes. Hell yes!"

He smiled. "I had a feeling you would. I'll give you his name and number, but I have a feeling he will probably be calling you soon. The clinic is set to open in two weeks. He's struggling to find qualified help willing to work in the clinic. I hate to say it, but some folks are just a little too uppity for their own good."

I grinned. "Not me. I have no problem getting in the trenches."

"I believe it. How are things going?" he asked.

It was a vague question. I wasn't sure what he was asking. "With?"

"Bree. How is she doing with the gallery? Really doing? She tells me it's all going great, but I worry about her. She can get a little hyper-focused on things. She did suffer a pretty serious trauma and I don't want her doing too much, too soon."

His care and concern were genuine. I felt no ill will towards Paul for trying to push her back with Nate. He loved his daughter and was doing everything he could to make sure she was happy. It was a foreign concept to me. I didn't understand that kind of love between parent and child. "She's okay. I make her slow down now and again. She does get an occasional headache, but I think that's par for the course."

He winced. "I hope she listens to you better than she listens to me."

I laughed. "Bree doesn't listen to anyone. I try to remind her that Rome wasn't built in a day. I remind her that she is only human and there is a lot more to living than working hard."

Paul nodded. "Good. I'm glad she has you. I know we've had our differences and I know you know about the situation with Nate, but she is thriving so I have to conclude that you are good for her. Bree is a high-spirited young lady. She needs freedom but she also needs someone that can ground her. I think that's you."

"I sure hope so."

"She told me she's actively looking for a house. I want you to know there is no rush for you guys to move out of here."

I smiled. "Thank you. I appreciate that, but at the same time I don't want to take advantage of your hospitality."

"It isn't like anyone else is using this place."

"Bree wants to buy a house. She wants to put down roots and make her own way. Hopefully, I will be gainfully employed soon and be a contributing member of this relationship."

He slowly nodded. "Money isn't an issue," he said. "Bree has more money than she could ever need. That's her money to do with as she wishes. My concern is that she is safe and treated right. If you can do that, I don't care if you have a penny to your name. Her happiness is my biggest concern. I can buy nearly anything. But not that."

"I will make her happy, sir. If I can't, I don't deserve to be with her. I love her and I will do everything I can to make sure she is taken care of. I will support her through anything that comes our way. She will be free to soar to whatever heights she can reach, but she will never be alone."

There was a softness about him when he talked about his daughter. "That's all I can ask. I've got to run now, but let me know what you think about the clinic."

"I will. Thank you for the referral."

He left me alone. I looked at my laptop and closed it down. I didn't have to look for a job anymore. It was a huge burden off my shoulders. With my morning now free, I decided to go back to the gallery location and see if I could be of any help.

On my way over, Austin called. "What's up?" I said. "I thought maybe you fell off the face of the earth."

He laughed. "I might as well have. I was in China working on some land deals. Things took a little longer than I expected."

"Did you make the deal?"

"Of course, I did. I'm Austin Hampton. That's what I do."

I smirked, shaking my head. "Always so humble."

"What have you been up to? Did you find yourself a job yet?"

"Actually, I think maybe I just did. It'll be working for a new low-income clinic here in Malibu."

"Oh shit. I wrote a check to that place a couple months back. I was beginning to think I had been swindled."

"Nope. From what I understand, it's set to open in a couple weeks. At least, that's what I'm told. I don't have an official offer yet, but I'm confident it will come through."

"Good, good. So, you told me a while back you were looking for a distressed property in the area. I think I found one."

My eyes got big. "No shit?" I asked with amazement.

"Yep. It's still going to cost a small fortune because of the zip code, but with some rehab, you could double the value in no time."

I grinned. "Shoot me the information, please. I'm really interested. I need to talk to Bree about it, of course, but she may just be on board with it."

"This property is beach front and it isn't on the market yet. I just happen to know a guy that knows a guy. So, we'll have to move fast if you want it."

"Can I see it today?" I asked, realizing there was no time like the present.

"Let me make a call."

"I'm open all day. I'll go talk to Bree about it right now."

"Sounds good."

It was what I had been looking for and had so far been unable to find. Bree didn't know I was looking, and I couldn't wait to tell her. I got to the gallery and spotted her right away. She was wearing a pair of heels, a short skirt and a shirt tucked in tight. She was meeting with an architect and said she wanted to make sure he took her seriously.

The only thing I could think about when I saw the outfit was getting it off of her. It was hot. Smoking hot. And she was mine. I stayed back, waiting for her to finish. She was talking with such excitement as she waved her hand around the huge space that she thought was a little too small. I wasn't an art critic and had been to exactly two galleries, so I was going to take her word on it.

She noticed me in the corner and waved. I winked, knowing she could see the action and earned one of her bright smiles. When she was finished, she sauntered towards me.

"What are you doing back here?"

"Watching you work. Is that weird?"

"Not at all."

"I got a job."

Her eyes widened. "No way."

"Well, I think I have the job. Your dad hooked me up. He made it sound like a sure thing."

"That's awesome! Congratulations!"

"Thank you. Are you free for the day?"

She shrugged a shoulder. "I was going to work on some paperwork, but I can be. What's up?"

"I want to show you something," I teased.

"Is that something big and hard?" she whispered.

I laughed. "Damn woman. Is sex all you think about?"

She softly giggled. "Maybe."

"It's big and I suppose it is hard, but it isn't between my legs."

She put out her bottom lip. "Well, that's too bad."

My phone vibrated in my pocket. I checked the text and saw it was from Austin. It was an address with the word 'NOW' in all caps. "We have to go right now, though. Can you?"

"I can. Let me grab my purse."

I escorted her back to my car and input the address in my phone. "I know you've been looking for a house," I started. "I might have found one, but there is one caveat."

"What would that be?"

"It's cheap."

She looked at me, one brow raised behind her sunglasses. "Cheap? In Malibu?"

"This is a distressed property. Austin gave me the lead. I have no idea what it looks like and I have zero information about it. But I was thinking, this is something I can help fix up. You know I can't afford the real estate here."

"Luke, we've talked about this. We're a couple and I want this to be our thing. If you aren't comfortable with it, we can rent a place."

I shook my head. "No. I've swallowed my pride. Most of it. But this is a chance to build something together. We can make it our own. It would be our little slice of heaven."

"I like the sound of that."

Rounding a corner, we found the address. I came to a slow stop as we both took in the house that was in desperate need of a paint job. The security gate was open. I had a feeling it was broken judging by the lean to it.

"This is it," I said.

"Can we go in?" she asked.

"I guess we'll find out." I headed up the cracked cement walk and knocked on the door. When Austin opened it, I was surprised. "What the hell are you doing here?" I asked.

He laughed. "I might have come by to see the place yesterday. I wanted to see if it is was worth your time."

"Is it?" Bree asked.

Austin grinned. "I believe it is. I'm not exactly a realtor, but I can give you the nuts and bolts of the place."

Bree clapped her hands. "I love it already!"

I looked around the huge entry way with holes in the walls and the once beautiful marble floor that was cracked and stained. It would be one hell of a project, but the more damage I saw, the lower I saw the price going. Bree was immediately in love with it.

Chapter Twenty-Seven

Bree

One year later

I WALKED OUT ONTO THE patio, a cup of coffee in hand. I stared out at the ocean. I was completely at peace with my life. I couldn't get enough of looking at the ocean. I had the images permanently embedded in my brain—just in case. Ellis assured me I was good to go, and my sight was good with no chance of losing it until the normal aging process gradually robbed it away. I planned on using every minute of my life filling my head with images I could recall when that happened.

"Hey," Luke said, coming to stand behind me.

I turned and smiled. "You're up early."

"I'm anxious for the day."

He laughed. "It's going to be a busy one."

"Can you believe this view?" I asked him. "Every day I come out here and I cannot believe we actually live here."

"Every day I wake up and can't believe you are next to me in bed."

I smiled. "I wouldn't want to be anywhere else."

"What time is Mel coming over?"

"She said she would be here by noon. I've got the food being delivered at one."

"I pick up my mom and Lisa from the airport at eleven," he said.

I nodded. "We have got a wild day ahead of us."

"Are you sure you want to do this? I mean, with just a handful of people?"

I turned to him. "Yes. This is my dream. I've always wanted a beach wedding. I've never wanted the big fancy party and the church. I cannot wait to be married on our beach."

"Our little slice of heaven," he corrected.

I smiled. "Our little slice of heaven."

"Your dad is still not thrilled with you bucking all traditions."

"He'll get over it. Like we said, there is nothing stopping us from having a big, elaborate wedding in the future if we want to. For now, this feels right. I want it to be intimate and special. I'm not interested in a wild party. I want our friends and family to be with us as we officially kick off our lives together."

He gave me a kiss on the cheek. "You don't think we've jinxed ourselves by seeing each other before the wedding?"

I laughed. "No. I don't believe in that stuff. It's a piece of paper. I already know I'm going to be with you for the rest of my days."

"And I know the same."

"Then the wedding and the traditions are all just extra. We know what we want."

"I want you," he said. "But right now, I need to get in the shower."

Watching him go back inside, I took one last look at the beach where I would soon marry him. It was going to be a very simple wedding. My dress was gorgeous. It was modern and hippie with a very classic, ethereal look that was perfect for a beach wedding. I had tried on the big princess style dresses and we had even started planning the big wedding when I realized I wasn't excited about it. I wanted to be excited about my wedding day.

Luke was on board with stripping it all away and just enjoying one another without the dog and pony show. I walked into the kitchen that had been completely remodeled. We were still working on a couple of the bedrooms, but the living areas were all finished. I smiled thinking of the many long nights we had stayed up, playing loud music and drinking beer straight from the bottle while we painted or laid new tile.

The two of us had become quite handy after about a million trips to Home Depot and another million YouTube videos. My dad couldn't understand why we didn't just hire someone to take care of the renovations. I had been skeptical at first, but Luke convinced me it would mean more if we did it ourselves. He was right. As I walked through our house, every step brought back a memory.

Like the time I had spilled paint all over the new section of floor we had just put in. We had laughed, well, I cried, then laughed and then we made love. It was one of the sweetest moments. I moved down the hall to the spare bedroom where my dress was hiding. That was one tradition we were keeping. He did not know what my dress looked like. I wanted to surprise him.

I thought back to the evening six months ago when we had been sitting on the patio after a long day of redoing one of the four bathrooms in the house. It had been a cool night and we had the patio heater on while we sipped wine. He had proposed under a starry night with the sound of the ocean in the background. I remembered every detail.

In fact, I had put the moment on canvas. It was going to be my wedding gift to him. It was a personal piece that would never see the bright light of a gallery. It was our moment in time to be cherished forever.

I took a leisurely bath, pampering myself and preparing for my special day. Luke popped in and gave me a kiss before heading to the airport to pick up his mom. I was praying she was as well as she claimed to be. She had been in intensive therapy for months. While she wasn't officially cured, she and Luke had slowly been rebuilding their relationship. I was happy for him, but ready to step in and save him should she fall back into her old ways.

Mel showed up and the next two hours were spent getting ready for the wedding.

"You don't look nervous at all," she commented.

I smiled at her in the mirror. "I'm not. I can't explain it. I'm just content. I'm excited, but not nervous."

"You are probably one of the few brides in all of history that is this cool."

"Maybe more brides should think about ditching the big show and just marry the man they love," I replied.

She laughed. "I'm happy it makes you happy, but when I get married, we are going to be popping tops and partying all night. I'm going to have at least two different gowns if not more. It's going to be in a castle with a million white roses and fireworks."

"You're nuts." I turned around to look at her, holding my arms out. "Well?"

Tears sprang to her eyes. "You look so pretty and so happy. I'm so thrilled for you. I can tell you this now because it's way behind us, but honestly, I thought you were going to die. I looked at you in that coma and listened to the doctors talking about the possibility of brain damage and I just thought I lost my best friend. I cannot believe you are standing here today, looking like a fairy princess."

Her words moved me. "I didn't think I would be here either. I was convinced my life would be spent in the dark for the rest of my days."

"And then there was Luke," she whispered.

I nodded. "And then there was Luke."

She blew out a breath, waving a hand in front of her face. "Speaking of, we should probably get you down there."

I took a deep breath and followed her out of the house. My father was waiting at the door to lead me down to the beach. "You look beautiful," he said, with tears in his eyes. "I'm so happy for you."

"Thanks, Dad. Don't let me trip on these damn stairs."

He chuckled, patting my hand that rested on his arm. "Not a chance."

I slowly walked down the stairs to the beach with all eyes on me. Luke was wearing a tux, something else I insisted on, with Austin standing beside him. Mel was waiting next to the minister we had hired wearing the gauzy pale blue gown we had picked out together. His mother and sister were sitting in their chairs.

My dad delivered me to Luke before taking his seat. I stared into the eyes of the man I loved with my entire heart. Our love had been born out of tragedy, which only bonded us closer together. We said our vows and sealed them with a kiss.

"Let's party!" Austin shouted.

We all burst into laughter and headed back up the long flight of stairs to our patio. I looked behind me and watched as Austin helped his mom.

"You look stunning," Lisa said to me once we were all holding champagne.

"Thank you, and thank you for making the trip over. It means a lot to Luke."

"I wouldn't miss this for the world. In fact, now that things seem to be settling down with my mother, my husband and I are talking about moving to Dallas."

"Really! That would be awesome. We'll definitely be able to see each other more."

She gave me a quick hug before moving on to grab a plate from the buffet that had been set up. I was taking a minute to take it all in when Charlene approached me. Things were still a little stilted between us. I had only seen her once since my visit to the hospital and it had been very brief.

"Hi, Charlene," I said, with a friendly smile.

"You're good for him," she said, taking me by surprise.

"Thank you. I love him with all my heart, and I will never do anything to hurt him."

She nodded. "I know. I'm glad he has you. I wanted to apologize for how things started off between us."

"It's okay," I assured her. "I'm happy you could come and want you to know you are welcome to visit anytime. We have plenty of extra rooms."

She smiled. "Thank you. I will be taking you up on that."

She drifted away. I sipped my champagne and couldn't stop smiling. Luke came over and gave me a kiss. "Are you happy?"

"More than happy."

"Good."

"Luke, I know you said you wanted to wait to take a honeymoon, but what about a short getaway?" I asked.

He shrugged. "I'm sure I could get a few days off. Are you thinking about somewhere up the coast?"

I grinned and slowly shook my head. "No. I'm thinking about somewhere tropical. Before you say you can't, you can. Your boss has given you the next two weeks off. Our bags are packed, and the tickets are in my purse."

He looked at me as if he didn't believe me. "Bree, what did you do?"

I giggled. "Surprise, we're going on a honeymoon to the Maldives!"

"No way," he exclaimed.

Everyone started clapping. Everyone knew about the honeymoon except him. He had been throwing himself into his work and then working his ass off on the house. He deserved a real vacation, something he'd never had before.

"Yes, way. We leave first thing in the morning."

He grabbed me, swinging me around. "I love you."

"I know."

He laughed again before putting me on my feet and giving me a kiss that left me blushing.

THE END

Blind Sight Series

Book 1 – See Me
Book 2 – Fix Me
Book 3 – Eyes on Me

Find Lexy Timms:

LEXY TIMMS NEWSLETTER:
http://eepurl.com/9i0vD
Lexy Timms Facebook Page:
https://www.facebook.com/SavingForever
Lexy Timms Website:
http://www.lexytimms.com

Lexy
Timms
Managing
BOSSES
Books 1-3
Lexy
Timms
FREE
for a
Limited
Time
BOSS
BOSS
BOSS

Want

FREE READS?

Sign up for Lexy Timms' newsletter
And she'll send you updates on new releases,
ARC copies of books and a whole lotta fun!

Sign up for news and updates!
http://eepurl.com/9i0vD

More by Lexy Timms:

FROM BEST SELLING AUTHOR, Lexy Timms, comes a billionaire romance that'll make you swoon and fall in love all over again.

Jamie Connors has given up on men. Despite being smart, pretty, and just slightly overweight, she's a magnet for the kind of guys that don't stay around.

Her sister's wedding is at the foreground of the family's attention. Jamie would be fine with it if her sister wasn't pressuring her to lose weight so she'll fit in the maid of honor dress, her mother would get off her case and her ex-boyfriend wasn't about to become her brother-in-law.

Determined to step out on her own, she accepts a PA position from billionaire Alex Reid. The job includes an apartment on his property and gets her out of living in her parent's basement.

Jamie must balance her life and somehow figure out how to manage her billionaire boss, without falling in love with him.

** The Boss is book 1 in the Managing the Bosses series. All your questions won't be answered in the first book. It may end on a cliff hanger.

For mature audiences only. There are adult situations, but this is a love story, NOT erotica.

Faking It Description:

HE GROANED. THIS WAS torture. Being trapped in a room with a beautiful woman was just about every man's fantasy, but he had to remember that this was just pretend.

Allyson Smith has crushed on her boss for years, but never dared to make a move. When she finds herself without a date to her brother's upcoming wedding, Allyson tells her family one innocent white lie: that she's been dating her boss. Unfortunately, her boss discovers her lie, and insists on posing as her boyfriend to escort her to the wedding.

Playboy billionaire Dane Prescott always has a new heiress on his arm, but he can't get his assistant Allyson out of his head. He's fought his attraction to her, until he gets caught up in her scheme of a fake relationship.

One passionate weekend with the boss has Allyson Smith questioning everything she believes in. Falling for a wealthy playboy like Dane is against the rules, but if she's just faking it what's the harm?

A chance meeting with one of the company photographers may turn into more than just an impromptu photo shoot.

Book One is FREE!

SOMETIMES THE HEART needs a different kind of saving... find out if Charity Thompson will find a way of saving forever in this hospital setting Best-Selling Romance by Lexy Timms

Charity Thompson wants to save the world, one hospital at a time. Instead of finishing med school to become a doctor, she chooses a different path and raises money for hospitals – new wings, equipment, whatever they need. Except there is one hospital she would be happy to never set foot in again—her fathers. So of course, he hires her to create a gala for his sixty-fifth birthday. Charity can't say no. Now she is working in the one place she doesn't want to be. Except she's attracted to Dr. Elijah Bennet, the handsome playboy chief.

Will she ever prove to her father that's she's more than a med school dropout? Or will her attraction to Elijah keep her from repairing the one thing she desperately wants to fix?

THE ONE YOU CAN'T FORGET

Emily Rose Dougherty is a good Catholic girl from mythical Walkerville, CT. She had somehow managed to get herself into a heap trouble with the law, all because an ex-boyfriend has decided to make things difficult.

Luke "Spade" Wade owns a Motorcycle repair shop and is the Road Captain for Hades' Spawn MC. He's shocked when he reads in the paper that his old high school flame has been arrested. She's always been the one he couldn't forget.

Will destiny let them find each other again? Or what happens in the past, best left for the history books?

** *This is book 1 of the Hades' Spawn MC Series. All your questions may not be answered in the first book.*

FORTUNE RIDERS MC
BILLIONAIRE BIKER
LEXY TIMMS
Download For
FREE
Lexy
Timms

MC
ONE YOU CAN'T
forget
BESTSELLING AUTHOR
LEXY TIMMS
Lexy
Timms
Grab Your
FREE
Copy Today!

A Burning Love Series

Book 1 – Spark of Passion
Book 2 – Flame of Desire
Book 3 – Blaze of Ecstasy

A Maybe Series

Book 1 – Maybe I Should
Book 2 – Maybe I Shouldn't
Book 3 – Maybe I Did

Darkest Night Series

Book 1 – Savage
Book 2 – Fierce
Book 3 – Brutal

Don't miss out!

Visit the website below and you can sign up to receive emails whenever Lexy Timms publishes a new book. There's no charge and no obligation.

https://books2read.com/r/B-A-NNL-PJMEB

BOOKS 2 READ

Connecting independent readers to independent writers.

Did you love *Eyes On Me*? Then you should read *Just Me*[1] by Lexy Timms!

We all need somewhere where we feel safe...

After leaving her abusive husband, Katherine Marshall is out on her own for the first time. She's hopped from city to city to avoid the man who made her life a living hell. When it seems she's finally found a new place where she begins to feel safe, she slowly grows confident that her life is looking up. A chance meeting with Ben O'Leary sets her life on a course and her soul on fire.

Ben launched a business that went on to viral success while he was in college, and now as a thriving entrepreneur, he's most interested in maximizing profits. A billionaire living the dream But all that changes when he sets his eyes on Katherine. Things between the two heat up

---

1. https://books2read.com/u/bP58Q7

2. https://books2read.com/u/bP58Q7

as they fall hard and fast—that is, until she gets an unexpected surprise that will test the strength of their relationship.

You & Me - A Bad Boy Romance

Book 1 – Just Me

Book 2 – Touch Me

Book 3 – Kiss Me

Read more at www.lexytimms.com.

Also by Lexy Timms

A Bad Boy Bullied Romance
I Hate You
I Hate You A Little Bit
I Hate You A Little Bit More

A Burning Love Series
Spark of Passion
Flame of Desire
Blaze of Ecstasy

A Chance at Forever Series
Forever Perfect
Forever Desired
Forever Together

A Dating App Series
I've Been Matched
You've Been Matched

We've Been Matched

A "Kind of" Billionaire
Taking a Risk
Safety in Numbers
Pretend You're Mine

A Maybe Series
Maybe I Should
Maybe I Shouldn't
Maybe I Did

BBW Romance Series
Capturing Her Beauty
Pursuing Her Dreams
Tracing Her Curves

Beating the Biker Series
Making Her His
Making the Break
Making of Them

Billionaire Banker Series
Banking on Him

Price of Passion
Investing in Love
Knowing Your Worth
Treasured Forever
Banking on Christmas

Billionaire Holiday Romance Series
Driving Home for Christmas
The Valentine Getaway
Cruising Love

Billionaire in Disguise Series
Facade
Illusion
Charade

Billionaire Secrets Series
The Secret
Freedom
Courage
Trust
Impulse
Billionaire Secrets Box Set Books #1-3

Blind Sight Series
See Me

Fix Me
Eyes On Me

Branded Series
Money or Nothing
What People Say
Give and Take

Building Billions
Building Billions - Part 1
Building Billions - Part 2
Building Billions - Part 3

Change of Heart Series
The Heart Needs
The Heart Wants
The Heart Knows

Conquering Warrior Series
Ruthless

Counting the Billions
Counting the Days
Counting On You

Counting the Kisses

Diamond in the Rough Anthology
Billionaire Rock
Billionaire Rock - part 2

Dirty Little Taboo Series
Flirting Touch
Denying Pleasure
Forbidding Desire
Craving Passion

Dominating PA Series
Her Personal Assistant - Part 1
Her Personal Assistant Box Set

Fake Billionaire Series
Faking It
Temporary CEO
Caught in the Act
Never Tell A Lie
Fake Christmas
Fake Billionaire Box Set #1-3

Firehouse Romance Series
Caught in Flames
Burning With Desire
Craving the Heat
Firehouse Romance Complete Collection

Forging Billions Series
Dirty Money
Petty Cash
Payment Required

For His Pleasure
Elizabeth
Georgia
Madison

Fortune Riders MC Series
Billionaire Biker
Billionaire Ransom
Billionaire Misery

Fragile Series
Fragile Touch
Fragile Kiss

Fragile Love

Great Temptation Series
The Devil's Footsteps
Heaven's Command
Mortals Surrender

Hades' Spawn Motorcycle Club
One You Can't Forget
One That Got Away
One That Came Back
One You Never Leave
One Christmas Night
Hades' Spawn MC Complete Series

Hard Rocked Series
Rhyme
Harmony
Lyrics

Heart of Stone Series
The Protector
The Guardian
The Warrior

Just About Series
About Love
About Truth
About Forever

Justice Series
Seeking Justice
Finding Justice
Chasing Justice
Pursuing Justice
Justice - Complete Series

Kissed by Billions
Kissed by Passion
Kissed by Desire
Kissed by Love

Leaning Towards Trouble
Trouble
Discord
Tenacity

Love You Series
Love Life

Need Love
My Love

Managing the Billionaire
Never Enough
Worth the Cost
Secret Admirers
Chasing Affection
Pressing Romance
Timeless Memories

Managing the Bosses Series
The Boss
The Boss Too
Who's the Boss Now
Love the Boss
I Do the Boss
Wife to the Boss
Employed by the Boss
Brother to the Boss
Senior Advisor to the Boss
Forever the Boss
Christmas With the Boss
Billionaire in Control
Billionaire Makes Millions
Billionaire at Work
Precious Little Thing
Priceless Love
Valentine Love
The Cost of Freedom

Trick or Treat
Gift for the Boss - Novella 3.5
Managing the Bosses Box Set #1-3

Model Mayhem Series
Shameless
Modesty
Imperfection

Moment in Time
Highlander's Bride
Victorian Bride
Modern Day Bride
A Royal Bride
Forever the Bride

My Best Friend's Sister
Hometown Calling
A Perfect Moment
Thrown in Together

My Darker Side Series
Darkest Hour
Time to Stop
Against the Light

Racing Hearts Series
Rush
Pace
Fast

Regency Romance Series
The Duchess Scandal - Part 1
The Duchess Scandal - Part 2

Reverse Harem Series
Primals
Archaic
Unitary

RIP Series
Track the Ripper
Hunt the Ripper
Pursue the Ripper

R&S Rich and Single Series
Alex Reid
Parker

Spanked Series
Passion
Playmate
Pleasure

Spelling Love Series
The Author
The Book Boyfriend
The Words of Love

Taboo Wedding Series
He Loves Me Not
With This Ring
Happily Ever After

Tattooist Series
Confession of a Tattooist
Surrender of a Tattooist
Heart of a Tattooist
Hopes & Dreams of a Tattooist

Tennessee Romance
Whisky Lullaby
Whisky Melody

Whisky Harmony

The Bad Boy Alpha Club
Battle Lines - Part 1
Battle Lines

The Brush Of Love Series
Every Night
Every Day
Every Time
Every Way
Every Touch

The Debt
The Debt: Part 1 - Damn Horse
The Debt: Complete Collection

The Fire Inside Series
Dare Me
Defy Me
Burn Me

The Gentleman's Club Series
Gambler

The Golden Mail
Hot Off the Press
Extra! Extra!
Read All About It
Stop the Press
Breaking News
This Just In

The Lucky Billionaire Series
Lucky Break
Streak of Luck
Lucky in Love

The Sound of Breaking Hearts Series
Disruption
Destroy
Devoted

The University of Gatica Series
The Recruiting Trip
Faster
Higher
Stronger
Dominate
No Rush
University of Gatica - The Complete Series

T.N.T. Series
Troubled Nate Thomas - Part 1
Troubled Nate Thomas - Part 2
Troubled Nate Thomas - Part 3

Undercover Series
Perfect For Me
Perfect For You
Perfect For Us

Unknown Identity Series
Unknown
Unpublished
Unexposed
Unsure
Unwritten
Unknown Identity Box Set: Books #1-3

Unlucky Series
Unlucky in Love
UnWanted
UnLoved Forever

War Torn Letters Series

My Sweetheart
My Darling
My Beloved

Wet & Wild Series
Stormy Love
Savage Love
Secure Love

Worth It Series
Worth Billions
Worth Every Cent
Worth More Than Money

You & Me - A Bad Boy Romance
Just Me
Touch Me
Kiss Me

Standalone
Wash
Loving Charity
Summer Lovin'
Love & College
Billionaire Heart
First Love

Frisky and Fun Romance Box Collection
Beating Hades' Bikers

Watch for more at www.lexytimms.com.

About the Author

"Love should be something that lasts forever, not is lost forever." Visit USA TODAY BESTSELLING AUTHOR, LEXY TIMMS https://www.facebook.com/SavingForever *Please feel free to connect with me and share your comments. I love connecting with my readers.* Sign up for news and updates and freebies - I like spoiling my readers! http://eepurl.com/9i0vD website: www.lexytimms.com Dealing in Antique Jewelry and hanging out with her awesome hubby and three kids, Lexy Timms loves writing in her free time. MANAGING THE BOSSES is a bestselling 10-part series dipping into the lives of Alex Reid and Jamie Connors. Can a secretary really fall for her billionaire boss?

Read more at www.lexytimms.com.

www.ingramcontent.com/pod-product-compliance
Lightning Source LLC
Chambersburg PA
CBHW070507160726
48003CB00004B/1464